THE
HAUNTED
HOUSE

Rebecca Brown

City Lights
San Francisco

Copyright © 1986 by Rebecca Brown
All Rights Reserved
First City Lights edition, 2007
10 9 8 7 6 5 4 3 2 1

Cover design: Stephen Guttermuth / double-u-gee
Text design and composition: Harvest Graphics

A Cataloging-in-Publication record has been established for
this book by the Library of Congress

ISBN: 978-0-87286-460-3

City Lights Books are published at the City Lights Bookstore,
261 Columbus Avenue, San Francisco, CA 94133

www.citylights.com

This book, with love,
is for my parents

1

THE DRUNKEN PILOT

"I'll fly, you navigate," my father'd say and we'd careen through Kansas City in search of Red's Pit Bar-B-Que. My father'd flop into the big old beat-up Ford and slam his door behind him. Then he'd lean his big arm over me and snap the map out of the glove compartment. He'd throw it on my lap and challenge, "Tell me how to get there, baby doll."

Each time we went, we had to go a different way, but we always started out the same. We left the brick house where my mother, my little brother Timmy and me, and our dog, Prince Lexington the Second, lived. We backed out of the driveway and headed right, then turned left onto Grand, then through the lights at Birch and Pine. I'd read the map, my head craning over the dash to see the street names in front of me. I'd try to find a new way we could go. But I always took us the wrong way, down one-way streets or onto roads undergoing construction. My father would yank the car around ("This baby'll turn on a goddamned dime," he'd whistle), and set us back on course. I could never remember how he got us out of these jams, but somehow he always did and we'd end up, just as I was about convinced that this time I'd really gotten us lost, pulling into the orange-lit open parking lot by the big red building. He'd screech the car to a halt and I'd bounce forward, slapping my hands against the dash. When he pulled the key out of the ignition the car shook and sputtered before it sighed and stood still. He'd leap out of the car before it stopped. I'd follow as fast as I could and try to imitate the big clangy sound he made when he slammed the car door fast and hard behind him.

Inside, the place smelled steamy and wet like red hot sauce and meat. My father and I ordered the same thing every time: a Big Red Deluxe for him and a Squaw for me, two orders of fries, a beer and a Cherry Coke. We'd go to one of the sticky plastic tables and he'd roll up the paper with our number on it in his hands. We'd watch the other people inside and watch the door when new customers came in. My father knew some of the regulars and they'd come over, slap him on the back and say, "Well hey, Commander, long time no see." They'd nod polite hellos to me.

Then they'd call our number and we'd go up to get our sandwiches, and carry them to our table on the ratty dark brown plastic tray. We'd unwrap the orange tinfoil and pull out the soft white buns with the red saucy meat inside. We'd salt the french fries and my father would put extra ketchup from the red plastic squeeze jar onto his sandwich. We'd eat fast, then wad the paper up into a ball. My father would toss the light shiny ball of trash over his shoulder, behind his back, into the garbage can by the door as we left. "Bombs away," he'd say with a wink, as the lid of the trash can snapped shut.

On the way home, my father would say, "Now *this* time," as if I hadn't every time, "*watch* where we're going." And I would recite the name of each street to myself after we turned: "Turn off Maple onto Poplar then onto Jefferson. Go down and turn on 18th." I'd try to memorize the route and come back that way next time. But I always forgot the way. Always.

I think of us streaming through Kansas City on those hot bright summer nights, the windows rolled down, the map crumpled on my lap, me watching my father's joy-filled face as he raced through yellow lights, barely braking at stop signs, lifting the tires off the road when he spun around a corner. This was his one joy with me when he came home. I don't know why he chose it.

We'd hit the driveway doing at least thirty-five, lurch over the hump from the street to the sidewalk and screech up to within an inch of the back wall of the unlit garage. I'd be holding my breath and holding my hands clenched tight and terrified on the torn plastic edge of the car seat. "Touch down!" my dad would shout, then wink at me. "Not bad for a foul weather landing." I'd stare at him with my eyes open wide, convinced we'd come within half an inch of our deaths. He'd lift the map from my lap, toss it back in the glove compartment, tap the door shut gently, almost preciously, then spring out of the car.

3

I'd follow him into the kitchen where my mother would be waiting, impatient and stiff, why hadn't we told her we were going to miss dinner, and he might think of asking her next time. I remember seeing my father's and my plates, the wilted canned green beans and chicken-fried steaks, the sticky coat on the lumpy circle of creamed canned corn, long since stopped steaming, the grease and butter coagulating into oily solid dots. I remember washing up after these meals with my father, him throwing the food, loudly and with great flourish, into the trash. My mother turned up the television in the living room to drown out the sound of our deliberate waste. I could practically hear her righteous silence and my little brother's quiet, wide-eyed cringing. These were the rare sharp times my father was at home. My father was a pilot.

* * *

My parents were married in Oklahoma City near the end of the Second World War. Because I've never known them to celebrate an anniversary, I don't know the exact year or date of their wedding. My father was in Navy ROTC and soon went to Asia. My mother says he never saw an active day of combat. My father neither affirms nor denies these stories, but I've never asked him point-blank. Like him, I've learned to mistrust fact.

He made a career of the Navy, and served it more than twenty years. Every two or three years, like clockwork, he got orders: my family had to move: Jacksonville, Milton, Norman, Kansas City, Kingsville, Monterey, Arlington. The towns and bases we lived in were small and backward and stagnant, full of military wives with kids and babies, desperate for quick and easy conversation over coffee and laundry, afraid to put down any root that would be torn up in another thirty months. Without the possibility of long-term jobs, the women worked at being wives. They threw parties every weekend. They watched sit-coms, traded recipes. They made hors d'oeuvres from Cheez Whiz and Velveeta. They talked about diapers and pets and household hints, anything to quiet the rattle of the transient lives they led.

But my father remembers little of these towns, because he spent near no time in them. His assignments were in the Pacific; he was "on tour." He'd meet us in the new town we'd just moved to, his new station, then leave for duty again. My father was not at home for any of my little brother's birthdays the entire time he was growing up. My little brother remembers this, though he does not remember the name of a single childhood friend.

Each time we moved, I swore that it would be my last. I'd get adopted or go live with the orphans at the church. But I always went, silent and cloudy, unable to keep from looking back at our oil-stained driveway, the small square yard, the tall skinny post of our government-issue mailbox. My mother tried to comfort me—"You'll make new friends in a few months, hon." But she stopped writing letters eventually, she gave up making friends. My father remembers nothing of these partings.

My father sent us postcards. From Turkey and from Thailand, Italy. And from France, Bombay, New Zealand. The postcards had pictures of camels and mountains, of women in tall high

5

hats. He wrote us, "Hi folks — the weather's hot. Found a great little restaurant near the water. Head for Tripoli tomorrow," signed it "Dad." Sometimes he sent us a photo of himself and wrote a caption, "Naples, April," "Biarritz, July." He couldn't ask us how we were because we couldn't write to tell him. His messages were always brief and caught between two places, neither of which was home.

"Home," my father told me once, "is someplace to go back to," then he sighed, "when you're tired of being out living." It's where he came to buy new socks and T-shirts, to stock up on chewing gum to take back to the natives. Did he ask us if we'd grown? I don't remember. I remember my mother measuring up three, four, five feet and marking them on a wall with a bright red pencil. Every two months my brother and I stood next to each other, our backs flat against the wall. I remember my mother's palm on my head, her voice, "Now stay still, honey," my brother's and my shoulders rubbing, us giggling, trying to stand on tiptoe. At first my mark was higher, but my brother's changed more quickly, then caught up with me, then a few houses later, stood above me.

When she knew he was coming back, my mother made a big run to the commissary. She bought steaks and baked potatoes, romaine lettuce, bottles of wine. She bought mixers and soda for my father's drinks. She checked the liquor cabinets to see how they were doing; they were always doing fine, the bottles untouched since my father's last visit home.

* * *

There's always more than you expect. Things pile up. You try to travel light but there's always something more you want.

My mother and I stand in the kitchen. She hands glasses down to me. I wrap them in newspaper then put them in a cardboard box. I cover them carefully. I want them to survive. Newsprint makes my fingers dark. I leave black ghosts of thumbprints, parts of palm, on glasses, silverware and cups. My mother tells me not to worry. I am mystified, but trust her.

My brother whines awake from his nap in his tiny room. My mother and I try to ignore him.

Every plate I wrap means something to me. This plastic one with the brown crunchy edge melted when I left it near the burner. This glass is all that's left of a set of four. Timmy broke two when he upset his highchair. I don't know where the other is. These forks and knives and spoons don't match. They're plain and scalloped and scratched. This one knife with the thick wood handle is always reserved for Dad.

We pack boxes full and tight, fold the sides up over the top and tape them down. Mom labels them "Kitchen — Plates," "Kitchen — Pots and Pans." We remove shelf paper, roll it up compact and stuff it in big extra-thick black plastic trash bags. I tie the tops with twisties. We throw out baking soda, yellow squirt bottles of ReaLemon, half-used jars of horseradish.

I follow my mother from room to room, sweeping the dusty floor where hairballs lived unseen for months beneath our furniture. My feet echo in the hollow house. I find crusty pens, a Ping-Pong ball, a lucky coin, a dog tag from a previous

Prince Lexington. It's the first time I've ever found things I'd lost and finally let myself forget. They're unexpected, precious. They're surprises. I feel, almost, like I've been given something. But it's more important than that; I now have proof things don't get lost, they all come back.

I feel tender toward dresses I find in the back of my closet that I haven't worn for months. I want to be kind to them, tell them I'll wear them and give them another chance. This whole thing's another chance, I tell myself. So this time I'll be careful, watch things closer. I won't lose track of things.

I want to stop my mother and show her. "Look, look what's here. I thought I'd lost this, but it's been here all along."

Each box I pack I look at things. I bought this comic book with Chuck at the PX. I wore this shirt to have my picture made. This half-done model airplane stopped when we ran out of glue. This shiny yellow shell comes from the ocean. It takes me hours. Everything I have becomes a treasure.

"How you comin', angel?" my mother shouts from her room. I look around my room and see half-emptied drawers, my closet shelves in shambles. When she walks into my room, she stares, open-mouthed, then laughs. "Robin, honey, you haven't done a *thing*." She sits down on my bed beside me. "You can't stop and look at everything."

"But I can't decide what to get rid of. I wanna keep my stuff." I wave my arms across the room at papers, a bag of string, my shells. She puts her arm around my shoulder. "I'm sorry, hon, but we've got to keep inside the limit. They can't move everything, you know."

She grabs a bunch of comics sitting on my pillow. "You've

got to learn to weed things out, darlin'. Here," she straightens the pile into a neat, square stack. "Choose your favorites and let the others go." Amazed, I look at her. She looks back at me, serious. I pull my shoulders up straight and give her one sharp nod. I swallow, lift the top one off the pile: *The Justice League of America*, the one with the story about how Mon-el and Shrinking Violet rescued the entire East Coast from an earthquake caused by invaders from outer space in cahoots with foreign communists. "Maybe I can give this to Chuck and ask him to keep it for me," I whisper. "That's a good idea," she encourages. "He'll hold it for you."

"And I can come get it when we come back to visit." My mother hugs my shoulder, then puts both her arms around me. She doesn't answer me, then leaves me to my task.

I make piles: things essential to me, which I must keep with me forever, things to store with my special friends, things to give my friends outright, things I can give to Goodwill, things to throw away. I tell myself this getting lean is good.

This stack I'll lend to Chuck will be another reason to come back. It's something tangible. My friends will think of me.

The first times took the longest. Things seemed important, almost permanent. We thought out hard each getting rid, each keeping. We believed we had a choice about our losses.

But every time got easier. Timmy helped and I'd learned what to do. We hurried through our tasks with the cool unthinking confidence of habit. Less and less we reminisced, sat down and sighed and called to the other two,

9

"Hey, look at this," when we found ticket stubs or snapshots crushed in backs of drawers. We learned that our remembering got in the way. We worked with growing silence. Soon we didn't talk at all.

Then my mother started what became a ritual. We'd move the couch out from the wall and plug the portable radio in. She'd turn it to my brother's and my favorite station, loud buoyant rock and roll, a station this radio was never tuned to in real life. My mother'd crank it up loud as if the adolescent anger in the troubled songs of love and loss, the crude songs of rebellion, would get us through this easier, help us forget. They did. We listened without thinking to the DJ's mindless patter about sunny skies and traffic snarls while speeding through our too-well-practiced work.

We taped up boxes tight. We labeled them fast with abbreviations we'd made up: K PnP, BR, Hall C. We stacked them by the door so we could load them. We scrubbed sponges over moldings, on the undersides of window ledges. Mom said, "This house has never been this clean before. They'll never know anyone was here." I learned to imitate the forced tone of my mother's edgy pride. Our home seemed like it never had been lived in.

Spurred by our memory of carrying so many things on previous moves, each time we threw out more. It became a challenge to see how little we could get by with. Discarding things became a snap. We knew that we could get another one, or at least something like it, but that we'd probably learn to live without.

Packing up took several days. Each night we'd sleep in lighter rooms. I imagined my closet shelves breathing clean, my dresser drawers dreaming of sunlight. On the last day, when everything was out, the three of us walked through the house, our feet slapping, the sun reflecting through curtainless windows, on the still wet, just mopped floors. The very shape of the house seemed changed, square and sharp and hollow. Everything was empty and blank and clean. We walked together, silently, without a word of memory.

In what had been the living room, the radio blared, its cheap rock echoing against the fake wood-paneled walls, down the hall, into dustless corners. The last thing we did was unplug it, and hear the last aborted phrase bounce, cut, surprised, against the bare bright walls.

Then the three of us walked out the front door together. I held the radio. Mom turned the lock. Timmy held Prince Lexington on a leash. Then, in Mom's words, "Just to stretch out before we sat all cramped up in the car forever," we walked around the block and encouraged the dog to pee. He jangled his chain at the end of the leash, looked up at us anxiously. He sniffed his familiar mailbox posts and trees and put his wet nose to piles of leaves. But he was always too nervous to pee.

I tried not to look at our neighbors' homes. The only words on these walks were my mother's worried mutterings; did she remember to disconnect the hot water heater, did she leave a tip for the paper boy?

When we got back to the car, Timmy and I flipped to see who had to start in the back on top of a suitcase, and who got to start in the front with Mom and help her navigate. Timmy was better at guessing the coin so I was usually hunched in back, my head craning over the boxes and bags piled up in the end of the station wagon, to watch our closed garage door fade, our small neat yard recede. Prince Lexington moaned in his travel box and we all prayed he wouldn't pee in the car.

Once the car doors were closed and she'd started up the engine, Mom spoke loud, her transparent cheer pretending this was just another outing. "We're going away on a wonderful trip. How 'bout a hamburger when we get outta town, you guys?" She put her foot on the gas like we were off on an adventure. The beat-up yellow Ford just lurched. She looked at Timmy next to her, then tried to catch my eye in the rearview mirror.

I learned early on that it was pointless to whine "Mom, I wanna stay." She tried to give us anything we wanted that she could. An Ultra-cheese Deluxe and fries, a triple shake and pie. Anything.

I swore to all my friends that I'd come back. I wrote them and remembered them. I would come back, I swore. Each time I moved I wrote the friends I'd just left, fervently. But my letters to the town two towns ago became less frequent. Then I became confused. My friends in Milton blended with my friends in Kansas City, then with people I had known in California. In my mind, I pretended my friends all knew each other. I'd ask for news of Mary Lou from Ellen. And only realize, when Ellen wrote back much later, that she didn't know any Mary Lou. I felt embarrassed, wrote awkward, apologetic letters trying to explain. I wrote them that it was too hard to describe on paper: I'd tell them how I'd got mixed up when I came back to see them.

In the new places, we did it in reverse. We swept and mopped and scoured things with Comet. Over the sound of the blaring new rock station Timmy'd found, my mother would shout, "I don't think those people ever cleaned this place the whole time they were here." Timmy brought in boxes, took them from room to room, yelling at Mom and me in the kitchen, "Which is my room again?" Mom and I unpacked and washed the kitchen stuff. We tallied up our losses: three broken plates, five glasses, one lost box of towels. We knew we wouldn't discover all our casualties until later. Only after we'd settled into this new imitation of a home, we'd want something, and realize it was gone — a spatula, a serving plate.

Prince Lexington whined in the bathroom where we'd put him with his food and water. "We'll let you out soon, honey," Mom shouted to his agonized moan. The dogs were always nervous when we moved. And though we felt bad locking him up, we all felt worse remembering the second Prince Lexington (or was it the third?) who got lost in one new town the day we moved and never found his way home.

But there were advantages.

In each place I could start again. They didn't know my failures and my shames. They didn't know the harsh things I had done to children littler than me. They didn't know about the times I'd been humiliated, the time Miss Ryder accused me of stealing the storybook, the time I'd walked Timmy to the bathroom when he wet his pants in assembly, how I'd dropped out of the spelling bee in the second round though Miss Hatcher was grooming me for the city meet. They didn't know what frightened me.

And for every friend I'd miss there'd be some lonesome awkward kid whom I was glad to leave. Some poor klutz who'd beg, like I begged the popular kids, "Just like me a little, you only have to be my friend for a while." Though I'd tell the lonely ugly kids, "I can't make friends with you; I'm moving," I didn't want to be told that myself. My always imminent departure was my way out as well as my despair.

I began to learn that truth takes time to catch up to a story. I could tell them anything I wanted. By the time they found out I wasn't a prodigy, a child spy, a rich and royal bastard, the daughter of a famous movie star, I'd be only a memory, if anything at all. I was a service kid in other children's lives.

I dropped suggestive, tantalizing hints, then I'd get silent. I'd make them beg to know my dark insinuated secrets. Then I'd keep them spellbound, rapt, spinning out unbelievable, inspired tales of the noble, tragic life my family led.

I said you were a hero, Dad. And in my grade-school world, that made me something of a hero too.

My little brother got quieter and quieter. I became his defender.

I marveled in classes in small southern towns when I met kids who were cousins, second cousins, second cousins twice removed. They knew each other's family histories.

No one knew if my clothes were secondhand. They'd never heard my jokes before. We were exotic. I could tell them anything. This was our strength, our right, our desperate protection.

I didn't tell them much.

We never went back to the old towns, Dad. My long, true painful letters to my fading friends were full of a promise I believed: that I'd come back. But it never happened, Dad. No one ever told me, "I remember you. You're home."

My father left the military in 1966. Again, the reasons for this are not clear. He was piped over. My mother and Timmy and I went to see the ceremony at the Navy base. We took the morning off school. Timmy wore a little suit. I wore my fancy dress.

We met my father at the base and walked with him to the hangar where the ceremony was to take place. I thought there'd be a lot of people there. There weren't. Besides the two other men in uniforms, who shook hands with my father, there were only four of us, my mother, my father, my little brother and me.

My mother and Timmy and I stood behind my father. My father faced the men. They said something to him. But we were standing in the wide open air of the airplane hangar with the wind and noise of departing planes around us. I couldn't hear. I stood straight beside my mother and I looked at my father's back. He wore his fresh white uniform. The gold braids on his shoulders shone. His shoes were black and polished, so black and bright they shone like light. The black rim of his cap shone too.

One of the men blew a tiny whistle, a pipe, then they each shook my father's hand.

Did I expect a cast of thousands? I think I did. I think I wanted one. This was my father leaving. Weren't his buddies here to mourn?

Then the two men shook hands with my mother and crisply turned away.

My father told us he'd see us at home later. He was going to the Officers' Club for a drink.

My mother drove home in silence. I watched her hands on the wheel tighten.

* * *

My parents and I watched the moon landing together. The three of us sat in front of the big color TV console in the big open den of our house.

When Neil Armstrong stepped onto the dusty gray-lined surface of the moon, my mother began to cry.

"I can't believe it," my mother said. She put her hand to her mouth and tried to laugh. "Isn't this silly. We put a man on the moon and I feel so funny." Embarrassed, and wanting not to make noise above the TV, she excused herself and went into the kitchen.

In a while the screen showed my father and me the earth seen from above. I saw the cloud shapes, white and beige, above our blue-brown planet. The world was tiny, and rung around with black. My father stooped in his orange corduroy armchair and sipped his glass of bourbon.

"Does it really look like that?" I asked him.

I tried hard to sound innocent, as though I still felt small and awed at the special things that only he could tell me. But even when I longed so hard to be innocent, and pretended to be so for him, we both knew that I wasn't. We knew he could no longer tantalize with his suggestive, half-completed stories of the other, richer life he led. My father was an ordinary failure, and so he told us ordinary lies.

My father didn't answer me. He just sat still, pushed into

the ugly orange armchair that had formed itself to the shape of his aging body. He sipped his drink and stared at the TV. I don't know what, if anything, he registered of the carefully humble speeches of the young and handsome hero astronauts.

After it was over and Edwin Newman came on, I went into the kitchen where my mother was just getting off the phone from talking with her mother. Mom looked at me and laughed as she wiped her eyes.

"I can't believe it, honey," she said. "The whole time I was a little girl I thought it was only a dream."

She tried to explain to me the magnitude of this achievement of humankind. But I wasn't awed. Ever since I could remember, there had been a space program with the goal of getting a man on the moon. My mother remembered the moon as a place of mystery and myth and wonder, completely unrelated to the real world. I'd never had her innocence about this.

"Grandmommy can't believe it either, honey. She *really* can't believe it."

We spoke in the kitchen over the repetitious drone of the TV commentators in the next room who insisted on the joy of this event.

That night my mother took me out in the backyard and pointed up to the sky. "I still can't believe it," she said. "We'll never be able to wonder about it the same way."

I asked her, "Does it look any different?"

She shook her head, "I don't know. I can't remember anything different."

That night as I looked up in the star-filled sky, like every other junior-high-aged girl in America, I made myself a solemn, silent vow: I would be the first woman to set foot on the surface of the moon.

Characteristically, I said nothing of this deep, true new commitment to either of my parents. Characteristically, they had managed to ignore one another completely throughout the entire event.

* * *

When I get to be the first woman on the moon, they put me on the covers of all the magazines and do interviews with me on TV. They tell stories about my humble origins, my pure good heart. They talk about my family. Edwin Newman comes to our cozy home to interview them. Mom wears a blue-checked dress and apron, Dad, a comfy cardigan, and Timothy, his college-letter sweater. They sit in the living room of our humble, comfortable old family home. My parents wear their house slippers. My handsome, confident young brother, now at State U, beams with pride and tells the American TV public he wants to be a doctor. They are all so proud of me. You can practically smell the just-baked freshness of the apple pie Mom has cooling on the kitchen windowsill. Dad grins with the pride of any middle-American, all-American Pop. They say they're "proud as punch" of their little girl, they "always knew there was somethin' kinda special 'bout her." Newman is sweet, if a little patronizing. "Oh, but surely you two are to credit for raising such a bright, ambitious girl." Dad and Mom blush and shuffle. "Well— shucks—" Mom shows him the photos of me from her albums, the blue ribbon I won in the sixth-grade spelling bee. The camera zooms in on the 5 x 7 portrait they have of me in my astronaut uniform, holding the American flag in my right hand, standing on the moon. The photo is signed, "To the world's greatest Mom and Dad. With love, Robin." I'm their special girl. We are our nation's darlings. Every family wants to be like us.

They passed out these forms at school one day that you were supposed to have your parents fill out if they worked in the aeronautics industry. It was something for taxes or the census so when Mrs. MacCammond asked whose dads worked at LTV, I raised my hand along with half the class. We were supposed to bring them back at the end of the week.

When I got home from school at three-thirty, my father was sitting, as he had for the past few weeks of his vacation, in his big orange armchair in front of the TV nursing a bourbon and water. I muttered "Hi," not wanting to interrupt his movie.

Mom, as usual, was in the kitchen, smoking a Salem and turning the pages of a mystery novel while she waited for something to cook. I pulled the form from my book bag and handed it to her. And then, because we were always conscious of not talking above the TV, Mom read the form in silence while I quietly rummaged through the refrigerator for something to eat.

"I'll give it to Dad when there's a commercial," I whispered.

My mother sighed, folded the paper neatly in half, creased it down the middle and exhaled. "Why don't you let me give it to your father?"

I looked over at her from behind the refrigerator door and shrugged my shoulders. "OK."

A few days later we were in the kitchen again. I found a bag of potato chips in the cabinet, then sat down on the barstool next to Mom and asked her where the form was.

She lit up a cigarette and blew the smoke out. "Your father doesn't work there anymore."

I heard the sound of the TV in the next room and understood why my father had spent his "vacation" sitting there staring at it, his fingers curled around his sweaty glass of whiskey. I wondered if he heard us talk. I reached across the counter and pulled the paper from between my mother's fingers. "Thanks for telling me," I said as crisply as I could. "You can thank Dad for me too."

I slid off the barstool and stood up straight. I looked hard at my mother. "Thanks a lot to both of you for protecting me so much. I really appreciate it," I said.

I stared at my mother and waited for her to say something. Then I walked back to my room the long way, through the living room instead of the den. I knew my father could see me heading down the hall. I knew he wouldn't look at me. And I was determined not to look at him.

My father had a variety of jobs after he left the military. The first was when he worked for an aeronautics firm selling aircraft or something. He had that one for a while, almost a year maybe, then quit or got fired. Again, this story has never been clarified, and it differs depending if it's him or Mother telling it. Then he worked on the road a lot. I think for a while he had something to do with a chemical company, then there was something with selling land. But all his work took him away from home and he'd check back into town every now and then for dry cleaning, etc. Then he was gone for good. Once he finally left, I don't think he ever worked again. He lives off retirement from the military and from some money that came to him from his father. He may have been buying and selling land in recent years, but again, I'm not sure.

The last Christmas before my father left:

My brother opens a pocket knife. My mother opens a new set of towels. I open a book about Anne Frank. From my mother, my father opens a bottle of Scotch.

My brother opens a basketball pump. My mother opens a new wire whisk. I open a first baseman's mitt. From my mother, my father opens a bottle of gin.

My brother opens a new T-shirt. My mother opens a new pair of shoes. I open a Monkees album. From my mother, my father opens a bottle of rum.

My brother opens a new capo. My mother opens a book on houseplants. I open a new pair of jeans. From my mother, my father opens a bottle of bourbon.

My brother opens a new pair of sneakers. My mother opens a pair of hose. I open a comb and brush. From my mother, my father opens a bottle of tequila.

My brother opens a mint set of coins. My mother opens a macramé kit. I open a tie-dyed shirt. From my mother, my father opens a bottle of rye.

After the presents, we clear away the crumpled paper and put our gifts into stacks beside the fireplace. My father's presents are all in tall square boxes, special holiday design.

Several times my mother had told us to let her buy his

presents. Having lost touch with our father, she had told us, we wouldn't know what to get him.

I remember the sound of the clinking of glass when I woke up that night to hear him packing his car trunk.

The next day there was a neat hole beneath the tree, the gifts that he'd been given, gone.

The day after my parents' divorce was finalized, I went to the principal's office at school to change my "personal card." I had to get a pink slip to be in the hall, the same pink slip you needed to get to be allowed to go to the bathroom. There was a place on the "personal card" that talked about your family. You checked boxes: Were your parents married, divorced, separated, widowed? Did you live with your parents, foster parents, guardians, relatives, friends? How many people were in your household? I checked off the new boxes and went back to homeroom. It took about five minutes. No one asked me anything.

"How do you know where you are?" I asked him.

"You reckon by the stars."

"And if the stars should move?"

"They won't."

But that very night, the stars all moved. The constellations lurched. My father's compass spun a thousand times. Cancer fought the Great Bear and the Dipper broke in two. The next day we all reckoned by a different set of marks.

When I was little, he told me, "Now don't cloud up and rain." And I wouldn't. I'd bite my lip and stare at him until my throat hurt so much I thought I'd die. I'd keep staring, silent, and think about my throat and concentrate on making the hurt go away, and when it was finally gone, I hadn't cried. Then I'd turn and walk away and hear him say behind me, "See, it's not so bad."

Each year the Girl Scout troop in Jacksonville had the Dad and Daughter Banquet. The first year they had it I got in a play and couldn't go. No one asked me where I or my father was. The next year I went away to camp. The third year my friend Kathy Schneider invited me to go and sit with her family. But suddenly, the day of the banquet, my father mysteriously appeared. To this day, I don't know how he knew it was Dad and Daughter Day. Nor do I know from where he drove to get there or where he returned to after the banquet.

You were supposed to let them know weeks in advance, but somehow I was able to get a place for my father on one day's notice. I called my friend Kathy and said my father was in town and I'd be sitting with him and she asked, "Do you want to tell me about it?" and I said, "What's there to tell?" When I got off the phone I was shaking.

I remember my fear when I went into the "banquet hall," the basement of the Methodist church. Kathy had come to my house for two years and never seen my father. "He works away," I'd mumbled, not knowing if it was true.

My father was handsome, though he looked older than I remembered. He wore a plain gray suit and pale yellow shirt. But in a way, he looked like all the rest of the fathers. I wondered if anyone else looked at him like I did, knowing how he didn't fit. We sat next to each other and I tried to point out my friends to him and tell him who was who. People came up and introduced themselves. Men asked my father about his work. I heard him tell them, "I'm an independent with a firm up north." "I handle a small portfolio of investments." "I'm a consultant."

He ate his greasy, pasty chicken without complaint. But when I saw him pull the fork toward his mouth, I knew this white and tasteless food, these useless chats with these fat boring men, the smell of all of us green-uniformed girls, were the reasons he had left. I watched him chew.

I tried to tell him what I was doing in school. We talked with Mr. Schneider and Kathy. Mrs. Cannon came up and said to my father, "I'm just so pleased to meet you, sir. Now I've finally met all the fathers of all my girls." Mrs. Cannon had peroxide hair and the biggest chest we'd ever seen, which was accented by the pink-stretch polyester pullover sweater she wore. Kathy and I thought she looked like a whore. She was rumored to have wanted to start our troop on a sex-education badge. In secret, we called her Boom Boom.

I watched my father smile graciously at her and say, "And it's a pleasure to meet you. I can tell you're working on getting all these girls into fine shape."

On the way home my father and I talked about what an awful person Mrs. Cannon was.

My father dropped me off at our house and didn't stop the car. I didn't ask where he was going. I didn't say, "See you later."

I was quiet when I got inside and pretended I was trying not to wake my mother, though I knew she was not sleeping.

She always stayed awake each night till I came home, and this night I wasn't even late. But I'd been with my father and I knew that, eager as my mother was to hear a confirmation of his failure and therefore my right, just hatred of him, she wouldn't ask me anything. For her half of our hostile pact, she pretended she was sleeping. I crawled into bed and tried to think of nothing.

There is a photograph. My mother and dad stand in line at a buffet meal. She's wearing a maternity dress and putting something on her plate with a fork. He's standing behind her, leaning over her, watching. His jacket is white and so stiff I can practically smell the starch crackling out to me through layers of brown and yellow on the photographic paper. His hair is thick and wavy and I think it must be blond, the color of mine. There is a shiny gold braid on his left shoulder. His buttons are crisp and black. Though in this picture he is leaning over my mother, watching her put food on her plate, I never think of this scene this way. I think of this picture in a way that it is not. I imagine his bright clear face looking directly into the camera, and to me. I imagine that he is smiling.

Three months later I was born. My father was in Asia.

"Where are we, Dad?"
    "We're flying."
    "What's that below us?"
    "Everything."
    "Above us?"
    "Only sky."
    "When will we be home?"

"We'll be there when we get there."

"Will you recognize it?"

"I don't know. I'll see something in the radar, a white dot blinking on and off."

"Is it different from the others?"

"Not really, no."

"Beautiful," my father says, "they're goddamned beautiful."

I stand next to him looking up at his khaki shirt billowing up and out in front of him as he looks through his binoculars. I see the glint of sun on my father's aviator sunglasses. I look up into the sky. Above us, half a dozen shiny planes, pointy and long and sleek, are tearing through the sky. It's a big blue sky with nothing even like a cloud for miles. We're watching the Blue Angels.

The planes make patterns in the sky. "It's art," he tells me, "goddamned art." His face lights up.

On the way home I watch him yank our old pathetic Ford in and out of gear. The car is noisy, a clunker usually used for grocery runs, hauling impatient Scouts across town to softball games. I watch my father's just-lit face go pale. His cheeks fall flat, his shoulders droop. He lights a cigarette. When the too-full ashtray spills, he swears, "Goddammit," mutters something else.

My father called me his little blue-eyed angel.

Every year the Girl Scout troop had the Dad and Daughter Banquet. The first year they had it, I got in a play and couldn't go. No one asked me where I'd gone or where my father was. The second year I went away to camp. The third year my friend Kathy asked me if I would like to sit with her dad at their table. Kathy was Catholic and she had five sisters. We laughed. "They'll never notice another one." I said OK.

The banquet was catered by a terrible local food service. We all wore our uniforms and ate greasy chicken with some unnamed beige sauce and overcooked carrots. We drank iced tea or lemonade and ate rolls and chocolate pudding. Our district leader, Mrs. Cannon, gave a little talk about how some of the fathers had taken as much interest in the troops as some of the mothers and wasn't that a wonderful thing. She told about how Angela Jackson's father took the girls up to see the fire department where he was a volunteer and how Mr. Benson had had the girls out for a field trip at the university swim department where he was a coach (and he even coached a girl who went on to be in the Olympics). These were stories of good, kind-hearted family-conscious men. Mrs. Cannon joked that all the mothers were home worrying that the dads would keep the daughters out too late and then what would we do.

Then, in the middle of the presentation on plans for the coming field trips, we hear a roaring overhead, the whirr of a propeller, the heavy thump of rubber wheels on the roof. The whole room sinks. We're silent. And into the room strides my father, breathless and panting, his long white flight scarf billowing behind him. He pushes back his flight goggles, tears his cap off his handsome head and tosses it neatly onto an empty chair before him. He sweeps over to me, where I'm sitting in my little green uniform by my friend Kathy, and takes me by the hand. He leads me over, in silence, to the two mysteriously empty seats near the podium in the front of the room where Mrs. Cannon is giving her little speech. Out from the kitchen, two cooks quickly wheel a cart with shiny silver-covered dishes. They whisk the cart to my father's side and I hear the clank of silver, polished crystal, china. My father exhales and smiles, points to the duck in orange sauce. The man in the white coat shows him the label of the wine bottle. My father squints, then nods. He leans to me and whispers, "Not the best year, but passable." The waiters gently lift crisp asparagus onto his plate. My father chooses the proper fork for everything.

When I turn to look at Mrs. Cannon, she's in military dress and it is wartime. She's delivering a speech to praise my father who is valiantly leading our troops in the war zone. She sings his praises, talks of his heroics. My father appreciates his meal with the wisdom of a connoisseur but eats intently, a man with little time to spare. I look at the long church basement tables in front of me, my friends and peers, the Girl Scouts. My eyes water with pride as they begin to applaud my hero father who took off precious moments from his immensely important work to come and be with us tonight, to sit with me.

My father made friends easily with strangers. With maître d's and bellboys, men he'd meet out hunting. He'd strike up talks with sons and dads on fishing docks and spend all day with them just trading anecdotes. He'd end up going out with them for barbecue and beer. "Great guy," he'd say about these sudden friendships. I knew that they would say the same of him. "Great guy, the Commander, helluva guy." In each new town we went to, my father seemed to know the bars and restaurants already. He felt at home in them, became a "regular" with his first drink. He remembered which waiter to ask about his sailboat and which to ask about his new shotgun. He remembered what his buddies drank and bought them all a round. He'd see them once or twice and not again. These were my father's friends.

My father and I fly from town to town, taking wings and flight, the sky, to simple country folks who've never even seen a plane before. His plane is big and solemn gray, mine's bright and red, a real plane, but it fits me like a glove. We are barnstormers. This is our America before my dad was born.

We fly to towns in the vast Midwest and set up shop for a couple of days, a few weeks. We take these simple folks above the sky to see their towns in a way they never knew. They're dazed and moved and altered. In every town some little girl or boy will beg us, "Take me with you." We are humble, kind, protective, tell them, "Child, it's no life for you. Go back to your good home." We pat their shaking shoulders, ease them back to all their moist-eyed mothers.

Families take us in and treat us like their own. They feed us good, old, passed-down recipes for chicken, apple pie and greens. They tell us that they love us and they ask us if we'll stay. But each time one of us, my father or I, will lean our hands against the table, push ourselves back, lifting up the front legs of the chair we're sitting in. We'll sigh, "Sorry, ma'am, but we're just not the stayin' kind. You been mighty good to us, but it's about time we're moving on." Then we help clean up our supper dishes by the solemn glow of dim warm candles and pack our planes by the light of the full Midwestern moon. In the morning we slip quietly out of the humble house before the good farm family is awake. We climb into our trusty shiny planes.

We know the entire family, Mom and Pop and all the kids and Rusty, the faithful hound, will tumble sadly and excitedly out of bed and rush to the porch in their long johns and nightcaps when the sound of our propellers cuts the peace of dawn.

We circle above the house, looking out over our wings to wave, and look at them looking up at us as we get smaller and more majestic as each second takes us higher. At first we can just make out the glistening tears in each of their crying eyes, then we can barely tell whose hand waves us good-bye the longest. Finally, their whole house is a small white square the size of a tiny matchbox, a speck, then something lost beneath a layer of cloud. Then we nod, pull down our goggles, give one another our serious, unsentimental thumbs-ups signal, and fly. We crank the throttles, lift the flaps and follow one another to the sky.

In the next town, we dazzle again, tell them stories they can just believe. We let them touch a piece of sky.

They tell us they will never be the same.

When we leave we fling our long scarves back, we shout "So long" and wave an open-ended wave. We smile with confidence. We leave them wanting, longing. The hearts we break remember all our gestures. We become their fantasies. They want to be remembered and they dream of our return.

* * *

I have a scar on the ring finger of my right hand, a tiny moon-shaped curl of white where I cut myself on a wind-up plane propeller.

You wound it up with your naked ring finger and you let it go at the exact right time. I watched you crank it up, counted the turns, watched the firm tight muscles in your forearm, your wrist. You patiently told me what to do. You held my hand. You said, "There's one exact moment when you have to let it go." You handed it to me. "You have to feel it."

I was careful. I counted the turns I gave to the rubber band. I held my tiny hands the way I'd seen you do. But I jolted, tried to hold it back.

The plane fell down, the propeller spun and cracked against the sidewalk. I remember the sound of plastic scraping in gravel, the sight of the sparks when the plane flipped over and over. Only a few seconds later did I feel the sting in my finger and look down to see the beautiful ribbon of blood running down my wrist, dripping onto the bright white cloth of my shorts. You snapped my hand up into the air and held it above me while you rushed me into the house. You pressed ice onto my hand and wrapped a white terrycloth washcloth around it. I remember our two faces in the bathroom mirror, me watching you press the cold wet cloth to my hand, me trying to figure out if your face read exasperation or concern.

From then on Timmy and I spent our allowance money, every penny our mother gave us, on buying model airplanes. We went to Ben Franklin's and pored over them, read as much as we could of the boxes' descriptions, looked at the pictures of the rugged, handsome men flying inside them, the turbulent skies, the tough terrain they'd conquered. Timmy and I pooled our pennies and quarters to buy the light, rattly sounding boxes, enamel paint, brushes with the tiniest bristles we'd ever seen. We bought tubes of glue. Timmy liked gluing the little parts of the plane together, putting his face right up to the bits of green and gray hard plastic, squinting till I thought his eyes would pop. My job was to soak the decals off. I loved the feel of the thin slick paper when it loosened, then finally gave and separated from the thick beige backing. I loved the soft wet feeling of my fingers in the water, gently gliding. I loved the warm, limp feeling when I lifted the decal from the sink and carried it carefully to Timmy's room where we spread the moist soft paper on the body of the plane.

We painted them. We named them. We held them in our hands above our heads and "flew." Running from end to end of the house, making what we thought were the sounds of flight, we swooped the planes in arcs, in delicate pirouettes and curves, deep dives, ascents, pretending we were flying, Dad, pretending we were you.

One night you go up in the sky. I see your plane hesitate, then there's a dark spot in the sky. When you came back, your palm is bright. It's like a jewel, a diamond pearl. You pick it out of your palm, pinch it between your thumb and forefinger. Then you hand it to me. It's a small one, but bright. It's one that I've been looking at for years. The path in the air from your hand to mine is an arc of silver glow. This is what you've plucked for me. It shines.

* * *

He says, "You must have faith in these symbols. You must believe what they tell you." I watch the red and green and blue dots blip across the dark glass screen. The radar line of white spins in a circle making gray-white shapes below it. "What does it mean?" I ask. He tells me clouds and water, fog. He says, "This is a mountain, that's a lake."

I never saw him like this. His skin smooth as a baby's, his hair full and blond, he's looking straight ahead. He's wearing a coat and tie, his shirt is white, his tie is dark and thick. His lips are full and puffed at once.

I don't know where I got this photograph. I cover parts of it bit by bit to see how much I'd need to recognize him. I cover eyes and nose, just leaving his full mouth exposed. I'm astonished. It's the most beautiful mouth I've ever seen. His chin is sculpted fine. There is a tiny rise between his chin and jaw. His nose is the most beautiful nose I've ever seen, perfect and aristocratic. But when I uncover his eyes and see his whole face, who he is, I cannot see his beauties anymore.

This is the man my mother fell in love with.

My father took me to restaurants. In each new town when he'd come home, he'd whisk me away some unexpected time to an unexpected place. I never knew how he knew about these places in out-of-the-way parts of town. They were small cafés run by brothers or foreign families, where everything was hot and strong, where they shouted in a different language in the kitchen. Where the barefooted kids of the owners came out from the back and stared at us, were shy and laughed and had dusty legs. My father knew what I would want and ordered it for me, explained what it was, took bites and told me, "This is OK, but I've had better." It was never food whose names I could pronounce, never anything I saw in stores.

* * *

My father blew into town from God-knows-where the week after my ninth birthday. He showed up unannounced near breakfast time. My mother made special pancakes and sausage and a pot of fresh-brewed coffee. She lit a fire in the fireplace. I made sure our glasses matched. I didn't let my brother use his special Mickey Mouse cup.

My brother and I ate slowly, conscious of our manners. My mother and father and I all talked politely. I told my father I'd just turned nine and I had had a party. I described the cake my mother made, the party hats and games. I told him the names of my friends and what they'd given me."

"Your birthday," I remember my father said, slightly puzzled, as if he didn't know what I meant. Then he winked across the table to me. "Well isn't that a coincidence, I might just have a little something for you myself."

When my father came in he hadn't carried a bag, but I knew not to ask about my gift. My mother had taught us, "Don't let on you want anything. Don't let 'em disappoint you."

At the end of the meal my mother said, "Now you kids clear up, then go play while your mom and dad have a little visit." She looked at my father and smiled. He nodded once at both of us.

Not one of us spoke as Timmy and I came and left the

room carrying out the dishes. But I remember being happy as I looked at my parents together, the way they both held their cups in their hands and blew steam off the surface of the coffee.

I heard them start to talk when I began to run the water in the sink. I tried to wash quietly, so the rattle of the dishes wouldn't interrupt my parents. But Timmy didn't open his mouth the whole time we worked. I tried to be nice, to scrub the big pans carefully and not splash water on him while he dried, but nothing I could do would make him look at me or change the stiff sad way his mouth was. When we went to our rooms, as I knew our mother wanted us to, I told him I'd read him a story or play airplanes with him.

But he just sat on his bed and didn't talk. He pulled away when I tried to put my arm around him. Soon I ran out of things to say to try to make him happy, so I went to my room. After a while I heard the clatter of my mother putting the coffee cups away and I started walking back to the living room. But then I heard the way their voices sounded. I hunched behind the door from the hall to the entryway. Through the cracks by the hinges, I saw my father's reflection as he looked at himself in the front hall mirror and combed back his wavy blond hair. My mother faced him and stared. He turned his cheek and looked at himself, then pressed his collar and made it perfect.

"I'll have nothing to do with it," my mother said. Her lips were tight and flat. "Do you hear me? Not a thing to do with it."

My father didn't look at her. He pulled his leather flight jacket from the coat rack in the hall and slipped it on. He continued to look at himself in the mirror, patted the outside pocket of his jacket. He pulled out his aviator goggles, blew on them and rubbed his hanky around on them in a perfect little circle.

"You'll *wreck* the damn thing," my mother said. Her voice was tight though she was trying to be quiet. "You'll get caught," she said, taking a step toward him. "God knows what could happen, you idiot. You idiot fool. The whole thing could go down."

I saw something like a smile flick across my father's face. He put his goggles on. Then you couldn't see his eyes. He looked up into the entryway light, then took the goggles off and rubbed them more. My mother crossed her arms across her chest. She glared at him and breathed out loud. Then she turned and started toward the hallway.

I spun around and ran on tiptoe back to my bedroom, flung myself down on my bed, grabbed a book and pretended to read. My heart was fast.

"OK baby doll, let's go!" my father shouted through the house.

I heard the angry shuffle of my mother's feet marching to my room. She swung the door open wide. "Your father is taking you out," her voice announced. "Here, take these." She went to my closet and yanked the warmest sweater, the big hand-me-down jacket from the neighbors across the street, my gloves, my scarf and woolly cap from inside my closet. It was late spring and I hadn't worn these things in months.

"Put these on when you get there," she commanded. "And strap yourself in tight, at least. Do you hear me? Don't let him bully you out of whatever scrap of safety you might have." She handed me the bundle of clothes and put her hands on my shoulders. She kneeled down and pulled me to her tight.

"Hey, come *on*, baby doll, let's go," my father shouted again. My mother dropped her arms from me and I ran to my father.

The front door of the house was open wide and bright clear light poured in.

My father stood alone in our front yard, his jacket zipped, his head leaned back. He was looking up at the brilliant white-blue sky.

I knew where we were going.

* * *

Up here we're over everything. Up here we're big as clouds. Up here we're far from everything, we're far from home, we're free.

Up here the trees all look like sticks and rivers look like ribbons. Up here earth curves like a thigh. Up here the air is white. Up here the fields blur, get clear, then crystallize to sharp. Up here we see where brown meets blue, where soil meets the sea. Up here we breathe what's sharper than the air. Up here we're everywhere.

"Up here, baby doll," my father shouts to me above the roar of the propeller, "you feel like you're almost goddamn free!"

I remember hearing, miraculously, beneath the roar of the propeller, the whoosh and monstrous whip of air, the creaking of his leather jacket when he moved. I remember sitting next to him, the side of his face, his rough red neck, the matted fur of the collar of his jacket. My father's hands gripped the wheel. I remember the whip of air on my face, the scratchy heat on my neck inside the scarf he'd wrapped around me. I remember clutching tight on to the belt that was clasped around my stomach. And mostly I remember the brilliant reflection of gold against his dark black goggles, the apricot glow of his cheeks when he turned us to the sun. His teeth were white when he parted his lips in something like a smile.

The instant I felt the ground again, my stomach clutched. I longed to be back up.

"When you grow up a little," my father said matter-of-factly, "maybe I'll teach you how to drive that baby yourself." He lifted me up and swung me from the plane. He spun me around above him in a circle. His mouth was laughing and happy below me, his eyes covered up by his dark sun goggles.

My body flew, my legs stretched out behind me. My hands clasped, thrilled and terrified, on his tense strong forearms. I remember I spun, I swung around. When he let me down, I stumbled, the world still spinning, brilliant, awful, bright.

They say that after you've had her, you won't want anything else again. They say you'll love her sleek shiny torso, the way she responds to your hands, that special tiny pressure of your thumb. They say you'll guard her jealously. They say you'll say to others, "You don't know." They say you'll love the way she smells and you'll take her scent home with you on your hands. They say you'll give her everything. You'll dream of her. You'll want her like you've never wanted anything before. Nothing else will satisfy you. You will not forget. They say that you'll get drunk and tell your buddies you've been with her. When you're with her you will see things that you never knew were there. They say you will come back to her. That even when you think you're safe at home, you'll want to be with her. They say she'll make you leave your home. You will. You'll do it gladly. When you're with her you will fly. You'll feel almost free, like you have everything. You will.

We time this flight the way you do in cities when you're trying to hit the green lights. We're heading for the horizon and it's dusk. We fly into the sunset slow. We're following the sun around the lip of the world, keeping in this line of pink and orange, this gauze of clouds at dusk. This time will be the closest we will ever get to time that will stand still. I watch my father in the pilot's seat. His face is pink like fire. And he is smiling.

* * *

My father jumps in the car and hollers at me, "We're blowin' outta this goddamn joint, baby doll!" I drop my baseball glove and run, jump into the car beside him. "Just doin' a little sightseeing," he shouts to my mother, who has hurried out after me. My father guns the engines and tears us out of town.

I sit next to my father. Dad's window is down, the hot Texas summer air blowing in on us. The radio's cranked up full blast, the tires screech. My heart races, thrilled and terrified.

"There's only one way outta this shit hole, baby doll, and

don't you ever forget it!" my father shouts at me above the roar of wind. "And that's to haul ass."

He floors the gas pedal at a yellow light, speeds through it as it turns red behind us.

"You know what that yellow light means, doncha?" my father roars, nodding back at the intersection we've just run.

"Proceed with caution," I recite timidly from my civics book.

My father laughs, "Come on, baby doll, what'd I just tell you? It means haul ass, baby." He looks at me, his foot pressed to the floor. "They can never hit a moving target, doll, never." He winks at me and looks back at the road.

I watch my father's head move back and forth, looking from me to the rearview mirror, then out to the flat gray stretch of highway ahead. I watch his face change, hard, then laughing, quiet and flat, the bright glint of sun through the windshield against the metal frame of his aviator glasses. And from where I sit next to him, I can see his eyes behind the lenses, the creases by the corners of his eyes.

We leave dry Tarrant county for the liquor store across the county line.

They didn't allow kids in the stores. We parked and my father leapt from the car and bounded into the store. I stood on the shallow porch beside the glass door and watched the wiggly lines of heat rise from the hood of the car. There were tough-looking kids hanging around the parking lot trying to get older kids to buy them beer if they gave them a couple of dollars. My father returned with a grocery sack, holding it tight in both his arms like a baby. I heard the clink, his arms careful not to upset or break the fragile glass.

* * *

We're in a glider, Dad.

You're wearing a light, airy polo shirt. It billows in the air. It's perfectly silent and we coast silently above the green sharp mountains of the Cascades. For some reason, it is completely warm. I watch you talk to me as if in slow motion. I watch the side of your mouth get lines. You make a joke, put on a foreign accent, throw your head back. Part of me knows I can hear you and part of me listens. It's like a movie with the sound track going on and off. I watch you in silence then, in slants of moments, I hear the story you're telling. I watch the propeller whirr around us and the solid earth below. We're both sitting on the wing, our legs crossed Indian-style. We're eating brown-bag lunches, sandwiches, potato chips and fruit. We drink orange soda from little green bottles. Drops hop above the sodas when you open them. We tap the bottles together in a toast. I don't hear what we say.

My father taught me how to drink.

It was South Texas where I went to visit him. Each summer I was in high school, I went for two weeks. My mother cringed and exhaled loudly through her nose for three days either side of these visits. Then she'd talk to me again.

My father started me off with beer and wine. Then we did the hard stuff.

This is what his apartment is like: there's booze in the den and on the shelves above the stove. There's booze in the basement and in the door of the fridge. There's booze on the patio and booze in the cabinet for booze.

He grabs different bottles by the neck and tells me, "This

is a decent bottle of Scotch, this is what you pour for your friends. This bottle," he reaches for another, "is what I keep around for unwanted guests." He laughs.

He runs his finger over shiny clean glass necks.

"Had a buddy in the Philippines, great guy, only drank Dewar's White Label. How the hell he got the stuff out there, I'll never know. Swore by the stuff. Medicinal." He winks. I see the wrinkles on his eyes. "Course, he was a limey."

Every bottle has a different story. The different shapes and colors shine. They ring with different pitches when he taps them. They are his anecdotes, his friends.

He tells me how whiskey's made, the difference in bourbon, Scotch, and rye. He gives me definitions: gin ("The limeys love it"); sloe gin ("Best-kept secret in the goddamn booze cabinet"); vodka ("Smells like nothing on your breath"); rum ("Kids and women drink it in Cokes and little drinks with umbrellas"). He tells me cognac, port, Drambuie. He pours me triple sec and Cointreau, makes me taste the difference. We watch pernod turn from clear to cloud. He tells me of the rise and fall of absinthe, shows me a bottle of tequila with a fat worm in the bottom. He pronounces martini "martin-eye," makes me a gimlet. He talks about the properties of little tiny onions and of olives.

He shuns after-dinner drinks, calls them "Liberace shots." The only one of them he'll drink, he says, is Kahlua. "At least south of the border they know how to keep a little kick in the damn stuff. Doesn't taste like a goddamn candy bar."

He makes what he calls "ladies' drinks" for me: grasshoppers, brandy alexanders, fresh fruit daiquiris, old-fashioneds. He tells me how to "build 'em." He tells me how to pick out bar fruit. "No refrigerator should ever be without a full supply of limes and lemons and oranges. You'll need tomato juice and soda, tonic water, and until your boyfriends grow up, Coke for rum and Coke. You'll need cream for the ladies' drinks and lots of ice. Here's how to crush ice." I watch my father's hands pull out a clean, unfrosted ice tray. He pops the ice out dextrously. He cups one cube in his palm and presses one in mine. He gets us two big tablespoons. The veins on his brown hands stand out when he grips the spoon tight. He whacks the round bottom of the spoon onto the cube and the ice shatters into beautiful clean shards of cold.

I imitate his action, splintering off a corner of the cube. I look at him, he grins, I try again. I lift the spoon up in the air and smash it down into my hand. There's the sound of a crack and the spurt of something broken in my hand. Dad grins. "There you go," he says. "Need to work on your aim, but you got the punch just fine." From then on, my dad will ask me, "How about a little ice, Robbie?" And I'll pop open a tray, just like him, crack the whole damn dozen of them, watch him divvy them into our glasses, watch the glasses gray with frost.

"But," he tells me once I've got it down, "of course when you're really drinking, and I mean seriously, you never drink with ice. You drink it straight.

"I don't like beer," he says. "I never drink it. Except for my one Carta Blanca in the morning. That's enough." He shaves over the kitchen table while he does the crossword puzzle in the morning. For breakfast he has a Carta Blanca, sometimes two. I remember the buzz of my father's electric razor, the round circles of water on the round glass tabletop.

I remember the recipes he taught me. Mostly, I make them

for my friends at parties. I drink my bourbon neat, straight up in solo shots.

I'm standing behind him at the duty-free store at customs. He's wearing a commercial pilot's uniform and he is handsome. His shoulders are wide and square and the navy blue, I know, brings out the deep blue in his eyes. Though I'm standing behind him, I know that he is smiling the jaunty confident smile the woman behind the counter will remember when they take their cigarette break. I'm several people behind him in line and he doesn't know I'm here. But he probably wouldn't recognize me anyway, because for some reason I'm dressed in a dowdy beige suit and sensible shoes. I look, I think to myself, like I'm a spinster. I don't know how old I am.

I see my father buy bottle after bottle of booze. He buys Johnny Walker Red, a bottle of J & B, two fifths of Old Granddad, a case of Dewar's White Label, a quart of cheap tequila. I stop counting. He puts the bottles in his one and only flight bag. It's smart and trim, efficient. I expect to see the bag get full — it doesn't. I expect the woman running up the bill to say, "You've gone over your limit." She doesn't. He keeps filling and filling the flight bag and chatting with the cashier, charming her. I stand on tiptoe behind him in line. Suddenly I've moved up several places and am standing right behind him. I try to look over his shoulder and deep into the bag below. When I stretch myself above him and look into the bag, I see it's black and deep and bottomless. I can just see the shiny, spinning glint of bottles as they careen down the bottomless well of his bag. They look like falling stars. And somewhere beneath the din of shoppers around me and the cheery ping of the cash register, the click of other people's bottles, I hear the spin of my father's bottles through air, down the deep black well of his flight bag. That's when I begin to feel I'm falling.

One night you go up in the sky. I see your plane hesitate, then there's a dark spot in the sky. When you come back, you open your palm wide and show it to me. I look up at your goggles and your flight scarf, the leather cap that's pulled down on your face. The only part of you I see, the rough growth of your two-day beard. I smell your breath and look down at your hands, now both of them, dark, open wide and deep. Dusty, dry as coal powder from coal. They're crumbling like ash. I think I hear you cough.

It's 3 A.M. I'm drunk. I'm playing poker. I'm visiting friends from college whom I haven't seen in years. We joke, we tell my lover Carrie that we all met "in the trenches." When the names of any of our former lovers come up, we growl with sympathetic anger, raise a toast. "To that old fucking war wound!"

When Davey's ex is mentioned, he flicks his cards up in the air. They fall around him like feathers, like confetti. One drops on his shoulder and he slaps his hand there, groans, "I been hit." He gags and rolls his eyes, falls from his chair. "Over and out." We all laugh at him like fools. From the floor, he waves a sharp salute to me, then drags his twitching body to the kitchen where he gets another six-pack. "Medicine for the troops," he shouts. We mock a solemn pose, then raise our cans together. "To all veterans of the fucking, shitting love wars!" We're loud and drunk. And, tonight, because we are together, we are happy.

My lover Carrie tries to laugh with us, at our dumb private jokes. But I have to break my laughter to explain things to her. And by the time I've told her the history of this joke, or who this character is, the punch is gone. It's just not worth it. Soon she tells us all good night and goes off to bed alone. Frankly, I'm relieved. I'd wanted her to meet my old buddies, but once we've gotten going, it's clear we're here to reminisce. We are ways with one another that we cannot be with anybody else. We're intimates because of our old history.

We tell again the tales of our green days "on the front." The mere mention of the names we called our profs gets us hysterical: "the Axe," and "Baby Man," and "Mr. Right."

We toast like cronies, try to hold our cards. But soon we're spilling more than we swallow. The hand ends when the two of us who have been honest have gone bankrupt and the other two of us are seeing double. Davey sways up from his seat and leans his arms down straight on the table. He looks at us through half-crossed eyes. "Well, troops," he starts, "we gotta go in there tonight and give 'em what we got. We gotta do it for. . ." Then he trails off and whispers, "What are we doing it for, guys?" We giggle. Janet shouts, "For the troops, Cap'n Dave, for us fucking loser troops!" Davey tries to stand, but topples. Janet catches him while Max and I try to stifle our laughter in our hands.

I think we toast and I think we laugh. Max leans across the table, shakes the beer cans and gulps the last swig from each of them. Then he steps over Davey and goes into the kitchen to make a pot of coffee.

I wonder if my lover will ask me in the morning about the scenes and ogres we described. Will she understand that the actual events that gave rise to the tall tales we all tell about ourselves are not the point? That our exaggerated, ordinary lies are our release, the way we cope with failure and loss?

Because later in the car, when Davey's giving them rides home, and I ask about Marie, Max tells me, "We're thinking about giving ourselves some time apart." He looks ahead, out at the dark in front of the windshield. I see his reflection in the glass trying to smile. When we drop him off he hugs us all good night. Always before we would have said, "And say hello to Marie," but this time it's quiet so Max says, "We don't fight or anything, it's just not like we thought it would be."

Next to me in the back seat, Janet leans her head against my shoulder, takes my hand and holds it. She kisses me and Davey when we drop her at her house. She tells me, "See you," as if she will next week. Then she turns to walk up the stairs. I hear her keys rattle when she takes them from her purse. I get in the front seat next to Davey. When we pull away, Davey starts telling me that Janet hasn't painted in almost three years, that her best work is still what she did our last semester. He say's he's stopped asking her about her job and she's stopped saying she's going to get a new one.

When we get back to his house we're quiet and careful not to wake his sleeping five-year-old or Carrie. We go to the kitchen and find another six. He points to the two big brown garbage bags full of empties, and giggles. We sit on the living room couch close to each other. Davey pops open the top of his can and tells me, "I mean, I know I drink a little too much.

Not *too* much, just a *little* too much." He smiles sadly and looks almost as pretty as he did when we first met.

Then he breaks into a grin that I don't recognize and takes a long, loud slurp of beer. And I do too. He tells me that he drinks a six-pack every night, not just on these "occasions." He tells me he's decided to stay at the store at least another year. "I'm afraid," he tells me, picking up the plastic truck his daughter has left on the couch, "and with the little trooper, I can't risk not having work."

I listen to the slow, deliberate sound the beer makes when he takes it in his throat. He nods his head in the direction of the room my lover's sleeping in. "It's good you've got each other," he says to me, "it's good."

Then he takes another drink and shuts his eyes.

Dad, we've never called our college years "the good old days." We don't have the illusion we were happy. We remember, accurately, that most of the time we complained. We saw ourselves as malcontents. We always thought, "When we blow outta this goddamn place — when we get outta here —" we'd do great things.

But back then, Dad, we still believed we could get out. We thought we could be free.

I think we thought our wounds were real, that they would give us wisdom, and the strength to leave. But they did not. They were only things that happened to us, stay with us, that we keep adding to.

"Dad, are you there?"

"Roger. Identify yourself. Over."

My voice is fuzzy.

"It's me, Dad, your daughter."

"Roger, I read you. Over."

"Dad, do you have some time?" I have to concentrate on every word.

"Oh-three hundred hours. Go ahead. Over."

"Dad, are you listening?"

"Affirmative. Over."

"Dad, I'm trying to talk to you." My voice begins to slur.

"Roger, we've established contact. Over."

"Dad, I don't think you're listening."

When I close my eyes, I'm dizzy.

"Negative, I read you loud and clear. Over."

I pause and try my hardest.

"Dad, we've got a Mayday here. We've got a fucking Mayday here at ground control, Dad." I stare at the receiving box in front of me as if I'll see his face inside the black shiny panel. The speaker crackles.

"That's not my duty. Shouldn't someone at HQ take care of that for you? Over."

"Dad—"

"Over and out. Over and out."

They say the Eskimos have a hundred words for snow. It is their life. It always is with them.

Plastered. Potted. Plowed, cracked, pissed. Tight, loose. One too many, had a few. Cranked, tipsy, tied one on. Ripped, looped. Seeing double. Intoxicated. Blasted, wiped out, blotto, high. Blitzed, smashed, under the influence. Rolling. Boozed up, tanked up. Juiced. Soaked. Sloshed. Trashed. Two sheets to the wind. Wasted. Wrecked.

* * *

My father's father died when I was young. I don't know if I remember him, or if I've just made up a memory from stories I've been told, a photograph.

My mother has pictures of when we visited my father's parents in Oklahoma City. I stand up straight and stiff, my arms stretched wide and flat on either side of me. I wear a white dress, red trim, the petticoats stuck straight out. I have on little black patent-leather shoes and my white-blond hair is a mess. My brother sits next to me and plays the clarinet. You can just see his too-tight tie and almost feel how stiff and hot he feels. I think that I am singing.

The one picture I've seen of my grandfather dates from before this time but I think of this time when I think of their house. We got dressed up ridiculously, even worse than Sunday, and we had grandkids' recitals. I can't imagine that either of my parents actually came up with these schemes and you can be sure neither Timmy nor I did. These afternoons of studied cuteness, these cavalcades of parodies of childhood, were my grandmother's invention. By this time, I now remember, my grandfather was dead.

The one picture I've seen of him is from an earlier time. It's color, but an early color shot. The colors run together, everything looks rose and slightly fevered. I think he was a gentle man.

The story I have heard of my father's father is this: he took care of his son, my father. He raised him. My father's mother wanted to become an actress. She wore tons of jewelry, lots of rings and earrings. Her hands were always heavy and made noise. Her hair, dyed bright and brilliant orange, smelled strong. Like perfume and like powder. She played piano, badly I'm now told, and directed like a duchess, which songs were sing-alongs and which ones were her showcase—where she was the undisputed star.

My mother says, with some contempt, "She never washed a dish in her whole life." She didn't shop or cook or clean; her husband did.

She left her family suddenly and ran off to New York to be an actress. She returned home within the year to settle down and preside over her salon, that is, her piano-studded afternoons with her out-of-town son and occasional friends. Her husband was her audience. Within a few years of the actress incident, she became a Catholic. And several years later, she died.

I'm sure of it now, I don't have a single memory of my grandfather. Just an impression, from scattered bits of stories and the smell of his wife's hair, what kind of man he was.

There is one story my father's told me, though. And though each time I ask for details I get fewer, this story is most clear to me. That one afternoon my father and my grandfather played clarinet and horn with Jimmy Dorsey. What Dorsey was doing in Oklahoma City or in my father's house, I've never heard. My father even says this was recorded. I've scoured record stores and catalogues to find rare recordings from Oklahoma City. There are none.

I misbehaved rarely. I was too shy a kid. But the rare times when I did act up, my father threatened me with being "grounded." My father explained that grounding was the worst thing that could happen to you. It's when they took

51

away your wings and didn't let you off base and you just sat there with nothing to do while your buddies were all out doing the real stuff. It was the worst fate you could suffer. They took away your freedom.

My father's opinions of cities:

"Naples is a pretty little city."

"Rio is the best damned restaurant city in the world."

"Corpus is picking up. Two great little Mexican restaurants and God knows the seafood is out of this world."

"Why any sane human being would live in New York City is absolutely beyond me."

"Saigon is the only city in the goddamn world where you can count on getting an honest cabbie —*if* you know how to treat 'em."

"The Parisians are god-awful, just god-awful. The only excuse for being in Paris is the food, and if you know where to go the best food is in the countryside anyway."

"Hong Kong is a hell hole, an absolute hell hole."

"London's nothing to write home about, but once the limeys have had a few pints, they can raise hell with the best of us."

"My God, do they know how to party in Sydney."

"Oklahoma City is the most godforsaken city in the country, probably the whole damned world. No one would miss the place if it blew up tomorrow."

"Rome? Fine for the first few drinks, but after that you could be in goddamned Tulsa!"

"Tell 'em the Commander sent you," he roars to me on the phone when I tell him I'm going abroad. He gives me names of restaurants and the names of maître d's. He says, "Just tell 'em the Commander sent you. Ask for Gino. Ask for Juan.

And there's a great little bar two blocks down where you can get an absolutely out of this world glass of —"

I listen carefully to my father, pause just the right amount of time, as if I were writing down the names of places in my own little black book of worldly things. But I don't. Going to my father's kind of restaurants isn't my style. And telling the maître d' the Commander sent me is certainly not my style. But my father wants to give me something.

I try not to remember the names of places, and most of the time I don't. But sometimes I find myself on a tiny street and recognize the name of a place, my father's description of a hand-done sign above the door, and wonder what would happen if I just stepped in and asked for Gino. But I'd be embarrassed — that they'd want me to be like him, to drink with them and spend the evening trading stories. Or worse, that they would not remember my father, and I would find that out for sure. Either way, I can't do it. Sometimes, I look into the steamy windows of these places, but mostly I just hurry on.

My father is one of the world's great hosts. He throws wonderful parties and makes his guests feel at home. Some of his pals will go nowhere else except "the Commander's place" on their time off. My father's fun. He makes great meals and builds great drinks and makes them feel like family. They envy his life-style. They say he's been around and, now that he's retired, deserves the good life. My father retired when he was forty-nine.

"Any idiot who calls flying commercial hard work doesn't know what the hell he's talking about," my father says. "It's a whole damned different ballgame." He speaks mysteriously and vaguely about the dangers of military flight, enemy lines, spies. "Does it compare, does it even *compare*," he asks, "with those candy-ass flights full of geriatrics flying down from Newark to Miami?" He sits at the table in his kitchen, gesturing with a sweaty glass. "A whole different ballgame," he guffaws, "a whole damned different ballgame."

My father says it's all in the relaxing. He takes me to the side of the plane where the big wide cavern of a window opens out to the earth below. He holds my forearm and yells above the wind, "When you've counted up, just take this cord and yank." He pauses, looks out to the ground, "I'll drop you somewhere nice, that green field over there." He points to a pasture far below.

When he eases me out to the blowing sky, I feel like I'm pushing myself through water. I float. I feel nothing against me because everything that pushes me from the outside is pushed back by the same weight from inside me. I uncurl my legs and urge my body horizontal. When I pull the cord, I feel the gentle whoop of silk billowing behind me. I pull my arms in front of me like swimming. I breathe in deep this rare and brilliant air. The only thing I hear behind me is the sweet whirr of his flight.

No.

No — when he pushes me out of the whipping sky, I yank the cord. It doesn't give. "You bastard," I think, "you bastard." My eyes bulge out in terror, anger, as I imagine him at the Officers' Club, looking tragic over his one straight shot of whiskey, telling them, "My little blue-eyed angel, the only thing I ever loved —" because I know the real story.

* * *

"Tell me how to get there." It's my father's slurred voice crackling on the shortwave. "Tell me how to get there, baby doll."

"What are your bearings, Dad? Over."

"I don't know," he whines.

"Where are you, Dad? Over."

"I don't remember, baby doll, I don't remember."

I sit in this tall light watchtower, staring at the radar circle, at the high beam searchlight that pans the fog, spreads its long greenish sword of light around me.

"Tell me how to get there, baby." His voice cracks, then fades. I'm losing him.

"Dad — give me your bearings," I whisper desperately. I grab the shortwave microphone tighter in my hand.

"I can't see anything —"

I hear the sound of the clink of glass against the throttle of his plane. Then a sound of a swig. I imagine his trembling wrist swinging the bottle high in the cockpit, his goggles crooked, the giant silver plane jolting in air. I listen to the fuzz, my father's open-ended radio, his cry, then fading into white noise, nothing, air.

My lover says my greatest fear is that I will become you.

* * *

I'm working as a baggage loader for a major airline and Dad is the pilot. I know where he's taking this flight, though they've tried to keep it a secret as I throw bags onto the conveyer belt and watch them rise into the belly of the plane above me. I know why I am here. I pull a special suitcase from behind me. It's heavy and I know that as soon as they're above the water, this thing will explode. As I feel my back tense and relax with my movements, heaving and pulling, I imagine the glorious spin of the snapped shiny metal, the huge exotic plume of black jetting into the crisp blue sky. I envision a burst of yellow and red, the sharp sparks of color blooming above the ocean. I imagine my father's crestfallen face when he hears the snap of the airplane's bone and remembers, finally remembers, who that girl with the bags reminded him of. He'll think of this as he falls, pirouetting like a ballet dancer through sky, then into the hard blue water, hard as slate below. His body will spin. From earth he'll look like an angel, a bright blue angel falling from sky.

He'll struggle with his parachute and not be able to open it.
Because I'm in his arms. He's holding me.
We fall.

The plane's lurch makes me weave like a drunk through the aisle. I pass out pillows and tell them, "Please put your head between your knees." It's my job to try to comfort this plane full of innocent people I don't know. I smile and hope my cute blue uniform cap's intact. In times of crisis, I tell myself, it's these little things that give us courage, and carry our belief that we'll survive.

But when I look down the aisle at the harmless, faithful passengers, I see they're all my lover. Every seat is filled with her. My lover in her old fur coat, my lover in the shower. My lover when we drove out West, my lover when we found the second cat. My lover naked, my lover scared. And each of her is screaming at me, "Get back in the cabin, you idiot fool! This whole thing's going down!"

Every one of her is strapped in tight by the seat belt. Each one of her is writhing, scratching to get out. I drop my jaw in wonder when I look down at my clothes. I'm not the sweet, shy stewardess I thought I was: I'm in my father's uniform. His trousers bag around my ankles, his sleeves stretch past my shaking knuckles. His leather jacket's heavy on my back. The air outside moves quicker than it's ever moved before.

The oxygen masks pop down from the ceiling and bob like toys on their plastic see-through cords. I stumble from row to row and tell my lover, "Please extinguish all your cigarettes." She screams, "Listen, you idiot fool, this whole thing's going down!"

But then her voice, her hundred voices go numb as the oxygen masks slip over her face. She's thrashing and struggling. Her body's clenched with the secret cramps of love that only I would recognize. I know that in her fear, her urgent need to send me back where only I can keep this plane from crashing, she will not concentrate on her own breath.

I watch, mute with honor, her last caught gag of breath make gray against the mask. I lean down over her, close as I can. I close my eyes and whisper, with the secret voice that only she would recognize, "Please return your seat back to the upright position." I wrap a hundred quilts around her hundred dying bodies.

While in the cabin behind me, I hear my drunken father roar. We are co-pilots.

I offer free drinks to all my dying lovers. I prop the pretty glasses in her limp and cooling hand. I announce to my lover, "We are sorry for any inconvenience. . ." And as the spin of the plane gets faster, the angle of our descent more steep, I think I hear her last gasp whisper, "Idiot fool, we're going down. This whole thing's going down."

* * *

This Christmas, out of kindness to our mother, Tim and I hide the gifts our father sent us. We don't open them Christmas morning but in a silent, private ceremony after Mom has gone to bed. We sit on the floor of my study, and after we've heard the calm pace of our mother's sleeping breath, we open the gifts from our father. I tear the package open, wishing the expensive crackly paper could whisper. I open a pink sweater, a box of chocolates, a tiny purse. These gifts aren't anything like me at all. I laugh quietly, "Well, *everyone* likes chocolates," and hand the open box to Tim. He picks one out and pops it in his mouth. He chokes. "They're all liquor." He swallows, licks his lips and laughs. Tim opens a shirt and an ugly tie. "*I* didn't get any chocolates," he whines with a grin, "gimme another."

Neither of our gifts has anything written on it, no note or card enclosed. They were gift-wrapped and sent from a store. Tim and I look at one another and try to hold our smiles. I look at my pathetic sweater and I'm touched; such a valiant, sweet attempt.

I picture our father in this big department store, embarrassed, asking some saleswoman, "Look, I have to get some-thing for the kids," her leading him through gifts that every son or daughter would feel happy with. Then I picture my father in his apartment alone, after his shopping trip, nursing a tall cold bourbon.

Tim and I look at one another, then he says with a laugh, "Hell, they're almost interchangeable. Neither of them will fit either of us." I cover my mouth with my hand when I start to laugh.

We tiptoe into my kitchen for a drink, trying not to wake my lover or our mother. We stay up late and talk and drink. At first we joke. And then I tell Tim that Carrie and I are talking about spending some time apart—I'm thinking of going abroad again. He holds me. Then he says, "I've got a special secret to tell you too." And he looks at me as sweet as when he was little, and he says, "Robbie?" the way he did when I was his Big Sister, he says, "Robbie, I'm not gonna bring any poor little baby into this world. I got a vasectomy." This is when we hold each other laughing.

Two stories about my father:

"Your father was on duty. Your father had been out drinking the night before and was in no shape to fly. His friend, your father's best friend at home here at the base, volunteered to cover for your father. And the plane went down. The commanding officer of the ship sent word back to me and I went to tell his wife. I told her and cried with her and tried to comfort her. Your father never said a word to her. Or to me. He never told her he was sorry her hus-band had died. He just forgot.

"Then it happened again. A few years later. This time he'd taken his time off and gone to the beach and gotten a terrible sunburn — you know how he burns. And his back was so bad he couldn't put his clothes on and his new best buddy took his flight and the plane went down. I didn't know this second fellow. Your father had just met him on duty. I heard about it from the commanding officer. Your father never said a word."

To drink, to leave, to not look back. Dad, this is what you taught me. To be a moving target, Dad. To lie, then to believe the lies we tell. To dream of flight.

But you never took me up, dear Dad. We never flew. That's just another lie I told myself. Your promise came to nothing, Dad. My foolishness is I believed that you'd come back. I think you thought so too.

Our sadness comes, dear Dad, because we believe the lies we tell. You wanted something perfect that would never die or change. Your wanted something, anything, to truly last forever, Dad, longer than your wasted life, longer than the lives of both your children. You wanted to outrun it, Dad. You told me something bigger and more glorious than truth, dear Dad. And I believed you.

But this is a true story.

He set me down on the edge of the pool and slid in the water beside me. The sound of his body was quiet and slick. Then he picked me up and gently eased me into the water beside him. He took my hands in both of his and stepped away from the side of the pool. He faced me, pulled my arms, out taut, took one step back to the center of the pool. Behind him, the water was still, the only movement, even ripples that went out from his body. Sun made rings across the clear green water.

"You can do it," he told me. "Just try to reach me." He pulled me from the solid side. I felt the water suck behind my skin. He squeezed my small hands tight in his. Then dropped me.

I remember the drop of his hands from mine, my desperate lunge for his suddenly distant body. I remember his stepping away from me, his garbled voice, as my head went under, "Try to reach me." I remember the brutal wet in my eyes. I remember the feeling of falling.

The water was heavy and everywhere, but nothing I could hold. I opened my eyes. His body stretched and waved like melting rubber. I kicked and opened my mouth to yell. I choked. His voice called to me from air. I yanked my head up, pawed. His hands were inches from me. I stretched out, desperate. I fell back again. I couldn't move to him. I came up almost close enough to touch. His arm stretched out to me. I fell.

Chlorine stung my nose and throat. My heart beat in my ears. My eyes burned. Everything looked waved. My father yelled above me, "Just reach out to me." I sputtered, fell. My legs were jelly, hands too small. I couldn't hold the water.

"Just come reach me," my father called. "I'm only this far away." His hands were always inches out of touch. I couldn't move. Each time I sank and rose more tired. I knew that I was drowning and I couldn't reach my dad.

Then, with the last drop of strength I had, I stretched to

where I thought he was and scraped against the rough edge of the concrete. I pulled my head up, panting. My father's huge hands grabbed me by my armpits, hoisted me out of the water, plopped me down on the hard edge of the pool.

"See, honey," he said, "you swam that far."

He pointed to the other side, across the frantic water I'd stirred up. I spat up water, gulped the thin good air, and felt my skin get cold.

My father put his warm big arm around me, hugged me close.

But that was only for an instant.

Then awkwardly, squarely, he placed both his hands on my shoulders, clutched them firmly as though they were bigger than they were. He laughed, "See, baby doll, what you can do? You crossed the whole thing by yourself." He nodded at the wide expanse he'd lured me across.

I remember the oily wet of his chest, the solid even ticking of his watch, his hands I'd tried so hard, and failed, to reach, around my heaving shoulders.

You're not a novice, you're casual. When the stewardess starts talking about the seat belt and the oxygen masks, you casually lean back in your seat and continue reading your novel. It's important to read a book rather than a magazine, especially the in-flight magazine. You have to look like you read every magazine cover to cover on your flight last week. You have to look like you own the place. You smile graciously with the stewardesses as if you're in with them. This flight is no big deal for you; how sweet and democratic you are to be charmed by the young flight attendants, the innocent country folk who are flying for the first time. You doze or pull out a legal pad and scribble numbers and equations. You look out the window occasionally and when the person sitting next to you says, "Beautiful," you nod and sigh, "Yes, it is," as if you are as familiar with this as with the acres that stretch from your back patio to the neighbors' land some hundred acres away. You are a traveler with mystery and season. You make friends easily with strangers. This is your territory.

The old man next to me buys me a drink. Then two. He asks me about myself. I don't say much. He gets another round of drinks. I hint I've had experiences in exotic lands, in Tripoli and Togo, Turkey, Thailand. I lean my head against the back of the seat, gaze out of the window with a misty, far-off look across my face. He asks me more about myself. I hesitate as if I'm telling him the truth. I tell him gorgeous, ordinary lies. He orders champagne, caviar. He asks me where my home is. I grin, "Everywhere."

He sighs and says, "You're free." I smile. He thinks I can't be tied. We toast. And then I tell him my opinions of cities. But he's an old man, he can't keep up with me. And soon, he starts to snore. I watch his fat jowls tremble and I look out the window. The lies I've told have made this old man happy. I finish off the bottle by myself.

I grab my two carry-on bags by the straps and leave the plane. The air at the end of the collapsible corridor is brisk. When I fling my bags across my shoulders, I lurch. It's only then I realize that I am completely drunk. I close my eyes and see the scene that I've just seen outside — the corridor and passengers, the luggage — inside my head, in negative and spinning. And then another scene of red. I snap my eyes open, stretch them wide. I stagger backward and hope these people will think my stumbling's from my heavy bags, my awkward readjustment to the ground.

I weave through what seems miles to the customs booth. I'm in a foreign country. The bag on my left is so heavy I set it down and stand there panting while I hold my breath. I close my eyes, then open them quickly again — the red scene is more clear — it's burning. The place around me is loud and spins. With the slow, deliberate logic of a drunk, I tell myself I just need one good shot to get me straight.

I sway into the airport bar, dragging my bags behind me, and buy myself a bourbon. I gingerly place my luggage at my feet and line the edges up straight, trying desperately to look like I am sober. I fold my hands over the cocktail napkin and sip my drink as quiet as I can.

From the spacious overlook window I watch the runway. It's evening and the lights are coming up. The sky gets pink then mauve. I'm tired, and my eyes are sliding shut. In the negative scene behind my darkened eyelids, the vision gets too clear: it's flame, a falling cone of light, a flash of silver movement. I force my eyes open and order another shot.

Outside, I see planes' smooth silver torsos like giant whales swimming in air. I watch, with envy, other people's partings. When I close my eyes, my whole head swims.

Because, dear Dad, this deadly mix of altitude and drink has done me in. I'm reeling, Dad. I'm dizzy. I can't stand.

And in the sad, bright, bitter clarity of drink, dear Dad, I realize that I cannot tell the myth from fact about you anymore. I don't even know what lies I've made myself believe about you, Dad. In honor, then, I raise this shot of booze to you. I drink one slug for me, then one for you. My chest burns when I swallow. I try to focus on the empty fuzzy space across from me. And, because I don't know where you are, I pretend that you are here. I raise my glass again and lie, pretend I hear the clink of your glass next to mine. I send this special toast with sadness, terror, hope, to you, dear Dad. I close my eyes and pray this toast will be a blessing, Dad, a hope for the beginning of a thing we could call love.

Years ago you taught me how to drink, dear Dad. Tonight, now, from your distant room, I think that you begin to teach me why.

Because when I close my eyes I see that flaming angel fall. And I know that I can't stop it. I hear the shriek of metal in wind, I feel the heat and choke on plumes of smoke. And I picture you, my father, your beautiful flying scarf around your neck, your leather jacket cracked with heat, your forehead shiny with sweat. I see your wet face, Dad, your aviator glasses melting, your deep blue angel eyes bulged out in agony and wisdom. I see your mouth about to open, Dad. You're almost saying something to me. I smell the liquor on your breath.

I see that silver angel fall again, again. It never ends. I want it to finish but it won't, dear Dad. It stays moving, motionless, caught in that searing, awful moment just before you're free, my father, just before your fierce and final landing.

2

MOM, THE MAKING OF A STAR

Before we left, my mother told us, "We'll see everything." She said, "It's going to be a different world."

I asked, "Where are we going?"

We cleaned out the refrigerator, took half-drunk cartons of milk, an opened box of Velveeta cheese, the remains of a bag of carrots, to our nextdoor neighbors.

We stood on their porch, where we hadn't stood since the day six months ago when we'd introduced ourselves. My mother handed over the bag of groceries.

"We're going away on a wonderful trip," she beamed. "We're going to see the kids' Dad who's in Italy. We'll show you slides when we come back."

They stood in the door and looked at us. When they said, "Won't you come in, Mrs. Daley?" my mother said, "No thank you, we've got so much packing to do." The screen door slammed behind us as we stepped off the porch. My mother looked up at the star-filled sky and said, "It's morning there. It's already tomorrow in Italy."

She sat Tim and me next to her on the big orange corduroy couch and opened up a book. She showed us pictures of old buildings, statues, ruins. She told us, "We'll eat pizza every day, spaghetti, whatever you kids want." She turned the pages reverently, and told us, "We'll see everything."

My mother sat between us. When the plane started rolling, she clutched Tim's and my hands tight. I watched her fingers tighten.

We sat still as our bodies left the earth. I remember the way my stomach pulled, the feeling of tight and full. I remember the feeling of falling, then the feeling of letting go. My mother stood up in the aisle and made Tim sit in her seat. She fastened her seat belt on him and pulled out her Instamatic. Tim pulled at the belt and whined.

"Smile, you guys, just smile for your mom, OK?"

I pulled Timmy up against me, forced my arm around him. "C'mon Tim, just smile once for mom, OK?"

She pulled out her notepad and wrote down everything, the food the airplane served us, the cities the pilot told us we were going over, the names of the people across the aisle. She asked them where they were going and told them, "We're going to Italy."

She wrote the names of both the movies they showed. They gave you things to put in your ears and turned out the lights. I tried to watch them both, but I couldn't keep my eyes on the screen. I kept looking out the window. I'd never seen the earth below — tiny and fast with pricks of light. I saw the lights of cities, then the clouds. I saw the lip of earth, the constant pink, the proof that somewhere, always, it was morning; somewhere different, it was always night.

But I kept looking at Mom, her joy-filled face. Her eyes shone bright when the screen was light. She held her hands together in her lap.

Her skirt and jacket, bought especially for this trip, were wool. She slipped off Timmy's and my shoes. ("You kids just get comfortable and try to sleep. It's going to be a long flight.") But she kept her shoes on the whole time, and her jacket, both hands on her purse in her lap.

I didn't sleep, but when Mom said, "OK, you two, let's quiet down," I closed my eyes and pretended, for her, that I slept. I listened to the constant quiet hiss of air, the quiet pad of stockinged feet. Sometimes I opened my eyes and saw the stewardesses chatting in the middle of the plane. The light was on above them. In their neat navy blue uniforms, they leaned across the counter and just chatted, like they were in a restaurant or at someone's coffee table. I imagined the way we looked from the ground.

I peeked at Mother next to me, pretending to be asleep, her head held high, her hands across her black purse in her lap.

Coming through the collapsible hall from the plane to the building, we looked for him. Turning into the baggage claim, we looked for him. Rounding the corner by the customs desk, we looked for him. We looked for him at the bureau de change, at the place where you hired a cab. At the information booth we found someone who spoke English. There was a message: the name of an apartment and a key.

Where did my father go when we were there? I still don't know. We always thought when we got back—from the market or museum, from a walk—that he'd be there. Maybe he was called away. But he would be there, we believed, waiting in the living room for us.

My mother cooked. She bought food, wine and fun things for the table. She cooked things she had never heard the name of. I remember sitting on the big stiff dark wood chair, the dark high back. I remember sitting in the apartment at our dark rented table, waiting.

While we waited for our dad, we used our time "constructively and wisely." Mom and I tried to teach ourselves Italian. We went through the apartment room by room, her Italian book in hand, and wrote down names of things on index cards, then put them on the things. Like *tavola* on the table, *sedia* on the chair, and *libro* on the books.

But mostly how we learned was at the movies. We'd see the same show more than once: English with Italian subs, then in Italian, English written in.

Thus, my mother took me to the movies.

Downtown theaters, late at night.

We took a bus. We sat next to each other on the gray-green plastic seat. The bus window was open and the air was warm and yellow. The outside lights flashed on and off, light—dark, light—dark, light—dark. Then long, long slides of light. The lights were yellow, green and gray. The bus rocked back and forth.

These warm nights were the summer when we'd come to meet my father.

My mother had on flats and hose, a bright white shirt and dark brown skirt. Her small hands held her shiny purse. Her fingernails shone they were so clean. She had a tiny bit of makeup on, a tiny line of dark beneath her eyes. Her eyes were blue.

If I stretched my toes straight down, I scraped the floor beneath our seat.

My hair was short, wisp-white and blond. My eyes were blue. The people on the streets called me an angel. They crossed themselves in front of us because they thought I was. At first I thought they only waved that way. My father called me his little blue-eyed angel.

The theater inside was huge and fancy. The tall red curtains looked like ribbons, golden tassels on the end. Girls walked up the aisles and stood down at the bottom of the room and sold candy. They had on little skirts and hats with words on the rims. I heard paper unwrapping all around me and smelled the sticky smell of apple candy, chocolate, sugary drinks.

When the lights went down, we gasped. I looked at my mom next to me. Her face was blue. I watched her neck, the white line of the surface of her skin. I looked around and saw the heads of other kids and moms, their faces blue and white, reflecting off the dimly flickering screen. The screen was wide and high, then bright and moving. We all clapped. In minutes we were caught. My jaw fell wide. For me, the whole wide world uncurled.

It ended when the people on the screen held hands and looked out at the giant sea, the giant brilliant sky. The clouds broke open. Sunlight streamed. They told each other gorgeous and true things. The final music surged up with a swell.

Outside, the air was sudden, cold and bright.

"You all right, honey?" It's my mother's voice.

I turn to her and nod.

"Well, let's get you something cool to drink, then we'll head back. I bet that poor nice girl is having a devil of a time getting Timmy to sleep."

Mom and I sit at an outdoor café. The tabletop is white and smooth. Above us is a big, wide, striped umbrella. The waiter brings us tall clear glasses piled up with ice, the round kind with the holes you stick your tongue into and suck until it breaks. He brings two bottles. He puts the glasses down on scalloped napkins, soft ones with gold print on the edge and Café Something written in gold. He pours my orange soda and her pure sparkling mineral water. I watch the smoky vapor rise, the sprizzles in the air. Drops hop off the foamy head. I pick my glass up with both hands. It's cold and I smell sweet orange, feel wet drops on my face when I bring it to my mouth. I breathe the wet sweet air and feel the cold wet in my throat. I close my eyes.

I think my mother touches me. I think she carries me, my sleep-drugged body heavy as a child. I think we're in a cab, alone. I think she holds me next to her. I think I sleep. I think I wake up in the dark. I think that I am home.

"Where are we going, Mom?"

We're on a train. It's night. But neither of us could really sleep because of all the stops we made and people going in and out, and Timmy waking, and of course, we were excited.

My mother said we'd meet "the people" on the train. She said it just that way, as if it were a new word we were learning.

We pulled into this station in the middle of the night. Everybody got off who was going to and we went and stood in the skinny hallway to get some air. Mom let me hold Timmy. Outside on the platform there were guys with guitars and tambourines. They had on black capes with colored ribbons — pink and yellow, green, light blue and red. The ribbons shone. They waved. They sang. They were "tunas," my mother told me. She was very excited and happy to see them because they were very traditional, traveling students who sang in groups. My mother told me this humbly, but proud. She had read about tunas in a travel book, and therefore had equipped herself to fully appreciate them. This proved that there was something to be said for her notion of preparedness in the world.

People clapped and smiled at them. Some people walking by gave them money. The air felt different coming in from the train station than on the train and even when the train was going in the country. I liked watching the people and wondering where they were going.

The tunas sang love songs and drinking songs. I could tell because of "amore" and "cuore" and "Vino! Vino! Vino!" They sang some songs looking up at Mom and me and Tim. They could tell how happy Mom was to see them. When they finished singing, some of them pulled out their boda bags and held them over their heads and the dark red wine shot down into their open mouths. It looked pretty and then one of them looked up at Mom and started talking to her through the train window. She listened for just a little bit, then she said, "Non capisco, non capisco." She yanked me and Tim back toward our compartment. I tried to listen extra hard. They kept talking, then shouting after us as we went in the train corridor. I heard them yell "Americana! Americana!" and "a casa" and other words. They were laughing too. We were walking in the corridor fast away from where they were outside. Mom kept saying, "Non capisco, non capisco," even though they couldn't hear us. I looked out of the train and saw them in the windows, rushing on the platform outside to follow our path inside the train. As Mom pushed me back into our compartment, I recognized the words.

"Mom," I said as she sat me down, "I understand. They want you to come to their house. You can sleep there with them." I heard them laughing outside.

"Non capisco," my mother said, as if she was saying it to me. "They're drunk," she muttered. She shut the door of the compartment quickly and pressed her hand on the door for a second.

"I understand what they said, Mom—"

"They're *drunk*, Robin—" she said, harshly. She pushed me back in the seat and looked at me sharply. I knew I'd better be quiet.

My mother breathed loudly. She pulled Tim on her lap and patted the seat next to her. I edged over and she put her arm around me.

I closed my eyes because, even though I wasn't sleepy, I

knew she wanted me to sleep. In a second or two, I felt the train start up and pull out of the station.

"Don't tell your father about this," my mother said.

I opened my eyes and looked up at her. "About what?"

"Any of this." Her voice was hard. "Forget this ever happened, Robin. Forget it."

Before we got there, Mom told me he'd have on his uniform and we couldn't hug him.

When we met him in Naples, his uniform was beautiful, brilliant and white and gold. The black rim on his hat shone in the sun.

My mother gave him her hand to shake. He did. Then he bent down and he shook hands with me.

MY TRIP TO ITALY
by Robin Daley

My mother and brother and I went to Italy to see my father. In Italy they have the Colosseum and the catacombs where they fed the Christians to the lions then buried them. Also in Italy are many pizza restaurants and ice cream which is not as creamy as ours but OK. In Rome, which is the capital of Italy, there are old ruined houses called ruins. Mostly they are columns. Italians are like us in that they drive cars and so forth. Other similarities are in dress. Differences are that most of them have dark hair. They have more churches than we have. They have Mary in the churches a lot because they are all

Catholics. The Pope also lives in Rome. The weather in Rome is hot, which is why there is so much ice cream. There are also many old ladies with fat legs who wear black clothes. Sometimes they hang out their windows and yell at each other. The streets are skinny compared to ours. They speak Italian which is faster and louder than English. I learned some Italian, not much. They seem to fight a lot. We went to Rome and Naples and Florence. There were movies with English written in. In Venice they don't have cars only boats because the streets are water though we did not go there. We took many pictures which I will bring in when they are done for show-and-tell. I would like to go back there someday because it was a nice trip.

These photographs became the punctuation of our family's life. My mother took them to the store to be developed. She sent some to him. "He'll want to see you grow." But each year she sent fewer out.

She put them into albums, with my help. She shone the slides on walls. The images were fuzzy — bright lozenges of light flung on the wallpaper, our shapes like colored ghosts in water, rising while she focused them, and then we'd straighten, all our outlines clear. She'd narrate, "Here we are at the Colosseum. That nice Italian lady took this one," "This is the house in Monterey." She stuck the photos in with tape, and then those special photo corners, and she labeled them: "Robin at 6 — Dad home between Malaysia and Laos," "Robin and Timmy, Dad before Naples," "Robin and Timmy, the Day It Rained, Kansas."

In most of these, my brother hunches, arms crossed tight across his body, his head bowed to his skinny chest. In all of these, my glasses tip. My mouth is half a smile, half a pained resistance to the sun or flash. My mother's hands are often on our heads, around our shoulders, trying to hold us in.

But it wasn't just the photographs she kept. I think my mother tried to hold on to everything, each little essay I wrote in grade school, the plaster casts we made of our hands in kindergarten. I think she had a need to keep the artifacts, the evidence that, rootless as we were, we'd had a life somewhere before, a place that, someday, theoretically, we could go back to, call home.

She kept the collar Prince Lexington wore in the Animal Day Parade in Kansas City, the snap of Timmy by the neighbor's wading pool in Milton. These proved that our existence was continuous. And too, they were my mother's quiet pride: "There you were, only in that school for three months when you won the spelling bee and got this cute ribbon." She kept the airbase circulars, "Newcomer wins AHS design award," "Robin Daley shakes hands with I. M. Pei."

These souvenirs were our marks on the wall. They showed how we had moved and had survived. They were words that Mom and Tim and I told ourselves over and over. They made us think we could remember us.

Sometimes we'd just be hanging out, doing homework together, or I'd have the paper and she'd be ironing, and she'd sigh. For a while I asked her what she was thinking, but then I tired to ignore her. I knew what she'd be thinking.

She'd say something like, "'Course Tim was too young to remember this, but you do — that crazy old waiter at that little restaurant who showed me how to squeeze that lemon rind into those little coffees? And how about that old fat lady who was slapping the pasta together in the back room? They were such happy people, such a happy time. . ."

I think she always wanted to go back. She dreamt of then, a place she thought we all could meet and all could be together.

But later, when there were other people, she changed. Whenever I tried to make a new friend or invite the neighbors over, she'd drag out all the slides and photographs, and pass them around. "Oh, it was such a lovely and delightful visit," she'd say stiffly as if she'd rehearsed it, forcing what was private on our unsuspecting guests. "My husband gave us the most lovely tour."

But gradually, her stories changed.

I listened to her tell people anecdotes of things that hadn't happened. I didn't stop her. I knew she wanted it to have been the way she told. I knew she told those lies to make us happy.

But when I asked her about other times, the most she'd ever do was nod, in half agreement, shrug reluctantly. She'd never offer anything herself. For each thing that she wanted to remember, was something else she wanted to forget.

I come home early from high school. I open the front door to the apartment and blink. I feel like I've walked into the dustbowl, but we're miles south of Oklahoma, and the dust is white and fine. I choke.

"Mom, what are you doing?" I cough toward the kitchen.

She looks up at me, startled, from behind a cloud of flour. Her face is wide, a huge open grin.

"Mom?"

"It-sa Momma Mia to-a-you-a, my lil' cannelloni!"

"Mom?" I rub my eyes, hoping I haven't seen what I think I have.

"O solo mio!!" she starts singing. She jostles around to my side of the counter and throws her fat doughy arms around me. "My lil' bambina, my lil' angelina mia, my-a own-a!"

"Oh, Jesus Christ," I sigh, trying to wrench away from her sweaty, unfamiliar grasp. She smells like olive oil.

She claps her fat powdered hands above her head. Her skin slaps against itself. She sucks in her belly, sticks her chest out and blares, "If-a you-a should-a go to-a Venice —"

"Mo-om," I whine, trying to bring her back.

Despite the fine flour coat that covers both of us, I see her skin is darker than it was when I left for school this morning. Her hair is greasy black and pulled back in a bun. Her sleeves are rolled up. She has a big mole on her cheek. Her yellow teeth, her garlic breath. She opens her mouth wide to sing.

"Oh God!" I shout, and grab her by her pasty shoulders. "Don't do it, Mom!"

I pull her face in front of mine and gag on a cloud of dry powder. Her eyes are deep dark brown.

"Oh my lil' rigatoni!"

Her voice is fat and wet. She pulls me in her arms again and starts us in a bearish waltz. For the first time in my life, I'm taller than my mother. I see the roll of thick flesh on her neck and the big mole at the base of her left ear. Her skin feels thick and soft beneath the coat of flour. I look down at her stubby, fat legs, where her pale calves should be. I want to push her back from me and yell. I almost do, but then she's hugged me tighter and I like the warm, wet feeling of her arms, the big soft cushion of her heavy breasts. I feel my feet start slipping in my shoes. My feet are growing smaller. Then, though I can't see it, I know my hair is getting light, to angel blond. I almost want to go with her, but I wrench myself away. "Goddammit, Mom—!" My voice rips out of me.

But she's still singing, clinging to me as if she hasn't heard.

"The streets are-a paved—"

I grab her by the shoulders and scream into her joyous face, "Goddammit, Mom, you're *not there*!! You're never going back there!!"

I dig my fingers into her shoulders and shake her. "Forget it, Mom," I spit. "For-get it."

Her face looks at me like I wasn't there. I shake her again. "Forget it, Mom."

Her voice is slow, "—with-a rivers. . ."

I almost recognize my mother's voice again. She looks at me, blinks. Her eyes are gray. She whispers, "And the boats glide up and . . . down."

I look into her sad blue eyes and say as clearly as I can, "Forget it, Mom. You can't go back."

She wipes a wisp of light hair from her face. And I see it's gray, not powder, that makes it look so colorless. I gently loosen my hands from her. She drops her hands down by her sides and looks over my shoulder into the kitchen behind me. I turn and watch the settling flour coat the cabinets, shelves, the top of the toaster. It looks like plaster dust in a house that's being renovated. I watch her hair turn gray, light brown, her breasts and hips start shrinking. She steps behind me into the kitchen. Her skinny, hunching shoulders droop. Her hands are slow. She starts water in the sink and wipes a sponge across the countertop. Neither of us says a word as we dump the half-made pasta in the trash. Neither of us comments on how many times my mother has to tie her apron tight around her feeble, shrinking form, or push her stringy, gray hair back.

That night, when I snuck from my room to the fridge, the tomato sauce tasted good.

When I peeked back into my mother's room, her body hadn't all come back. I tiptoed to her bed. I stood above her face, and in the ash-gray light, I looked at her. Her skin still had an olive tone, her hair a tint of black. I tried to see the moment when her wrinkles reappeared, her deep Italian tan went pale.

When she opened her eyes and looked at me, I caught my breath. Neither of us spoke or in any way acknowledged that we watched each other in the awful dark.

Because she never mentioned it, I thought, perhaps, that she had been asleep. I doubted that, but I knew I would never know unless I outright asked her. Perhaps she thought that she had dreamt. Perhaps she has forgotten.

We never spoke of this.

I think that's when she learned how to forget.

My second year at UTA, I applied for a scholarship to study abroad. I had to write a little essay about why my proposed study of domestic architecture was worth their putting their faith (read: money) in me. I suppose I was fairly honest about my interest in architecture and the importance of studying it where it all began, but frankly, if I'd felt like going to Tahiti, I'd have told them I was interested in grass huts. The point was, I wanted out. Because the real point was, Arlington, Texas, was boring. And it had been boring from day one. But when the days started adding up, it became absolutely excruciating.

Mom encouraged me. "You gotta go out and be your own person, honey. Don't stick around this deadbeat town. Go see the world. Don't let anybody hold you back. If your momma says go, you go. I'm so proud of you, honey, that's my girl."

And Mom was right. I needed to have my own life outside of this stagnant, backward suburb. I'd have all sorts of experiences when I came back. I told her I'd come back.

The scholarship people also wanted an essay from a family member. Getting Tim to write papers for his remedial English class was tough enough, but getting him to write about his family would have been a joke.

So, of course, Mom wrote the essay.

She could have sent it straight to the scholarship people. I didn't have to read it, and frankly, I didn't really want to. I didn't want her to say something different about me because she thought I'd see it. But she wanted me to read it. Actually, she wanted to read it to me.

It was Sunday morning. Every Sunday Tim went out and played ball with the Big Brothers and Mom and I ate frozen honey buns and watched TV. She'd set up the ironing board and iron while I sat in the big orange corduroy armchair and read the paper. We kept the TV on low and heard, beneath the rustling of my paper or my Mom's unconscious, happy hum, the drone of Edwin Newman's voice. When I found something interesting in the paper, I'd read her a headline. "Oh, that sounds good," she'd say, "read it to me." Or, "Too depressing, let's have the funnies." Then I'd read her the comics and she'd make faces like the scenes I described. Sometimes one of us would look up and actually watch whatever was on TV, but mostly we just kept it on as background, softening the silence between our words. When Mom was nearly done ironing, I'd go fix her bath — the exact temperature and amount of suds — and she'd step into it right after she'd ironed her last shirt. Sometimes I'd sit in the bathroom while she soaked and read her the rest of the paper.

But this Sunday was different. Tim was out with the Big Brothers, as usual. The TV was on too, and I sat in the orange chair and turned through the paper. But the paper sounded really loud. Because Mom wasn't humming at her ironing. She was in her room writing her essay about me.

I turned the TV up. I felt like if I could hear the scratch of her pencil, that even though I couldn't see what she was writing, it would be like eavesdropping. I watched Edwin Newman interview this guy from the Middle East for twenty minutes and I didn't hear a word.

Then my mother came out of her room. I heard the door open. There'd just been a commercial and the show was going again. I pretended I was deep in the program. My mother didn't interrupt me. She sat on the couch and put her reading glasses on. She read her essay to herself. I sat in the orange chair and pretended I wasn't watching her from the corner of my eye. When she finished reading, she came over to my chair. I looked up. She smiled down at me with her quiet, not-wanting-to-interrupt smile, and leaned down to pick up the parts of the Sunday paper that were lying at my feet. Then she went back and sat on the couch and rustled through the paper. I felt my mother sitting across the room pretending to read. Then there was another commercial and I didn't know what to do.

"You wanna hear what I wrote?" my mother asked.

I scraped at the leftover frosting from the honey bun on my plate. "You don't have to read it."

"I know," she said.

My mother had just started up at UTA in the Speech and Drama department. She'd always wanted to be an actress, but there was always something else she needed to do — take care of me and Tim, and Dad when he was home, get a job after Dad kissed off. In other words, she was always living for someone else, always waiting for some other time. But when I got the scholarship to UTA and started working part-time at the housing project, and Tim got in with his group, she was able to cut down on her hours at the store and go back to school for a few courses.

So she did, and sometimes we did our homework together. She'd recite her lines to me and I'd clap and comment and boo like a crowd. We called me her "adoring public." I made popcorn, ate it loudly, crunched up candy wrappers while I watched her. I'd laugh when she was funny and I'd sniff when she was sad. I'd moan exaggerated sighs as if she were the star she dreamt she was. I'd make her think that she could make us feel anything. I told her someday she'd be rich and famous and I could say, "I knew her when."

So when she turned down the TV and cleared her throat, it was almost something we were used to.

Though not quite.

"My Daughter, Robin Daley," my mother read, "By Betty Daley."

It sounded so strange when she said her name and mine, the way it does when you meet someone else with your name and you call them that, but can't believe its the same name as your own.

My mother's reading glasses slipped down her nose as she leaned over the page. Her hair fell over her glasses. I looked beneath her reading glasses and saw her eyes. Her voice was clear and slow. I watched her hands against the page.

My mother read to me about our family. She acted out the parts. I saw her mime my brother's walk, his face when he was young and always pouting. My mother acted out my life. She played herself and me. She wrote about me like I was her dearest friend. My mom read words that opened me. I remember the moment she said the words.

When she was done, I watched Edwin Newman on TV, the way his mouth moved and the mouths of the people he interviewed.

Mom and I both watched the silent, animated screen move with the words we couldn't hear.

She said, slipping off her reading glasses, "So, what do you think of it?"

I didn't know what to say. Already, my mother referred to what she'd said about me, in the abstract — an "it."

"Well, should I change any of it? Are any of the sentences unclear? Did any of it get awkward?"

"I—" I cleared my throat. "Not that I noticed."

"Hmmmm." She put her glasses back on and looked at the papers. "Well, maybe it wouldn't be ethical for you to get so involved in this essay about you, huh?"

"Yeah," I mumbled.

My mother straightened her glasses again and looked at me over the rim.

She stacked the papers neatly, all their edges square. She took her glasses off, folded the earpieces back and carefully placed them right side up in the center of the pages. She leaned back on the couch and faced the TV. I turned the volume back up.

I think we were relieved to save ourselves from looking too closely at those bold, bare words, the sounds that said the feeling that my mother had for me.

When you say a thing out loud, and to someone, it's different from not saying it, or saying it alone. It means you give it body. Saying makes a thing between the listener and speaker. It means it's not a secret any longer. But also, it becomes a thing itself, a thing that stays a thing itself, aside from listener or sayer. And that's the part that's magic, terrifying, the part that stays beyond forgetting or remembering.

"So," my mother said, "my little girl is leaving." She smiled as if she was happy and proud. I smiled back, self-conscious, prouder than I meant to be.

"I'll come back," I said.

I saw the wrinkles near my mother's eyes.

My mother's essay named a thing in us. The words she

said became a pact, a thing between us, over us, which we would never look directly at. But still that thing moves in through us. It stays in us, inheres.

And too, my mother's essay was my ticket out. I got my scholarship.

Thus I made my first return to someplace I had been before, alone: to Italy.

I step off the plane and I'm back. Outside I smell familiar smells I thought I had forgotten. The cats that eat spaghetti in the Colosseum, the shapes of ladies in black. The buildings are tall. They're old and new. The streets are wide and high. All the men are handsome and the women — like movie stars. I get drunk on Chianti, Soave, the freedom and the fear of me alone. I order food because it sounds vaguely familiar, smile when my plate appears and I recognize a dish. I stand quiet on buses, trains and listen to their accents. The shape of the sky behind the tops of bell towers, the scent of olives and wine. The kids have dirty knees and all wear shorts, dark blazers, school uniforms. I watch their black shoes on the streets, their manners in a bar. I watch them play ball in the parks. I find restaurants and I ask for Gino, Juan. I pass old movie theaters, huge posters with the names of stars. Every street brings something back. I find myself downtown and lost. I turn. I don't know where I'm heading, wander into someplace else familiar. I walk the city. I take trains. It's all the same, as if it had been waiting: proof.

I send my mother postcards from abroad. From Turkey and from Thailand, and from France, Bombay and Naples. I send her recipes I learn from women in the kitchens of cafés. I tell her family secrets they've passed down from mom to daughter, generations. I send my mother anecdotes, half-truths of my adventures, while I hint of tales more wondrous than I tell. I want to make her think that I've grown. I want to make her think that I've forgotten.

Arlington, Texas

Dear Robin honey,

The most amazing thing has happened. Remember that awful "Star Search" contest they have in Fort Worth every year? Well, a gal I was in Speech and Drama with won this year's contest and some director from a big Hollywood studio saw her and decided to cast her as the ingénue in his new film. The movie is a rags-to-riches story in the best (worst?) Horatio Alger tradition, with a little Norman Rockwell thrown in for good measure. Anyway, this director got some bee in his bonnet and decided to hire a bunch of unknowns to give the film that edge of authenticity. And I'm one of the unknowns. The publicity ploy is absolutely transparent to me, but I'm not complaining. It's great to have work.

Anyway, they say we'll be filming for months, so I'm taking an apartment on location. Tim wasn't able to come help me pack, but I was real careful with all your stuff I had to put in storage. You can decide what you want to do with it when you get back to the States.

I hope you'll come stay with me before you go off someplace to work (did you ever get a response from that firm in Chicago, by the way?). I won't nag you about living close to your poor old Mom anymore, but it sure would be nice to see you. I miss our little times together. I'll send you my address when I have one. Stay sweet, angel.

> XX,
> Momma

My plane arrives from Rome at 2 A.M.

I look for her.

Coming through the collapsible hall from the plane to the building, I look. Turning to the baggage claim, I look. Rounding the corner by the customs booth, I look. At the bureau de change, at the place where you order a cab.

I step outside, knowing I'll see her double-parked in the loading zone only, our old beat-up Ford clogging two lanes of traffic. I look for her.

She's caught in traffic, I tell myself.

She'd sent me articles, had warned me that the place had changed, grown big and cosmopolitan. I knew it would, but I close my eyes and tell myself it hasn't much. I squeeze my eyes tight and stand there in the hot dry air and breathe it back: the red clay underneath the steaming asphalt, dust, and tumbling tumbleweeds. I can almost hear the stomp of far-off hooves of cattle, horses, buffalo. I smell the oil wells. I open my eyes. I look for her.

The sign above the taxi stand reads, "Welcome to Dallas–Fort Worth International Airport"—I chuckle to myself—"and welcome home."

I look for her.

A man on the sidewalk next to me wears boots, a black felt cowboy hat with a line of sweat where his brow has stained the flannel. He moves slowly, lanky, a bowlegged amble, throwing luggage into the open back of his pickup truck. On the front seat, a woman with bouffant hair died blond holds their tiny son in his tiny Tony Lama boots, on her lap. Her cowpoke husband eases into the driver's seat beside her and pulls off.

I look for her.

And step into the airport bar to wait.

I push in through the swinging doors of the Longhorn and grin at the garish, overdone, plastic "authentic Western" decor. The waitress with peroxide hair asks, "What'll it be, hunny?" For a second, the traveler's instinct that had made me try the vino di casa in every little out-of-the-way town I wandered through Europe, tells me to order the local specialty, which here would be a Lone Star longneck and a plate of nachos. But I'm not just going to be here for a visit, I remind myself with happiness; I'm under no self-imposed obligation to sample the local stuff. I can order my standard, which I do: "Shot of bourbon and a water back."

"Thank yew, hun," my waitress says, her good, familiar accent warming me as much as my whiskey will. I sit by the window in full view of the lobby. I know I'll see her walking up, too fast for the length of her legs, her big sloppy purse sliding down her arm as she waves, "There's my baby! There's my girl!" and breaking into a full, floppy run.

After I finish my second drink, I begin to worry. She's never been late before. I leave my table and dial our number from a phone box. The phone rings twice.

"We're sorry, the number you have dialed has been disconnected. Please check the number and dial again." The voice is a recording.

"Thanks for telling me, Mom," I mumble to myself. I dial the operator.

"What city please, hun?" Her leathery accent perks me up like a smell of a bowl of four-alarm chili.

"Arlington."

"Thank yew, go ahaid."

"I need a listing for Betty Daley on Woodland Park Boulevard."

"Hold on a second, hun, I'll check for y'," she says as if she's patting my knee.

I look out the phone-booth cubicle to see if she's coming. I can imagine so clearly her tumbling through the crowd, her big purse slipping down her arm, all a-twitter because she's late.

"No Betty Daley on Woodland Park Boulevard." Her voice has changed, efficient.

"Pardon me?"

She's crisp. "There's no Betty Daley on Woodland Park Boulevard."

"You sure you got it right, Wood-land, not Wood-lawn."

"I had it right the first time, miss." She's brusque now, almost hostile.

"Uh . . . any B. Daley on Woodland Park?"

"Nothing."

"Any B. Daleys at all?"

"Look, miss. I got no B. Daley's anywhere. You want Bob, Bill, Bruce, I got 'em. But I don't have any Bettys and I don't have any B.s."

"Um . . . how about Elizabeth. Or an E. Anything there?"

"Lady, you get two inquiries per call. This has been more than that and your party isn't listed, got it? You sure you got the right town?"

I stare at the phone, then out at the empty crowd in the airport.

"I don't—"

The other end of the line goes click.

"I don't know," I mutter to myself. "I don't know."

I step out of the phone booth and head back to the bar.

"Excuse me, sweetie, there are no minors allowed in the bar."

My waitress stands in front of me with her tray full of drinks. I can smell the shot of bourbon inches from my face.

"But I'm—"

She winks at me. "Come on, you can't expect me—"

I reach in my pocket to pull out my wallet and show her my passport. "Oh shit," I mutter, "fucking shit." Because it's not that suave Italian linen I had worn on my homeward flight, but the faded tie-dyed bellbottoms I wore in high school.

"Fucking shit," I say again. My bangs fall into my eyes the way they haven't since I was fifteen.

"Well . . . I—I left something in the Longhorn," I stammer.

"The where?"

"The Longhorn." She gives me a puzzled look. "The bar," I insist. "Can't I go back and get my bags?"

"You really can't go in there, miss," she says, eyeing my Monkees T-shirt. "How did they let you in there in the first place? You can't be more than—"

"Look, will you get it for me? I was sitting by the window. It's a big Italian leather shoulder bag and canvas tote bag."

She shrugs her shoulders. Nervously, I watch her wind into the bar. And that's when I notice, through the smoky air, that the decor has changed. The garish longhorns teetering on the mantelpiece, the barbed wire replicas hanging on the wall are gone. Ferns hang from baskets in the ceiling.

"Jesus Christ," I moan. I turn around and hope my mother will find me before it gets worse.

"Nothing in there, doll," the waitress says when she comes back. "But I brought you a little something." Thank God, I think, as she lowers the tray to me, I could use a stiff shot. But it's rose and pink and settling at the bottom of the glass.

"A Shirley Temple," I say halfheartedly. "Gee, thanks."

"You OK, sweetie?" She puts her arm around my shoulders protectively.

"I'm — I'm waiting for my mom."

"Is your momma in the bar, little girl?"

"Christ no," I whine. "She doesn't drink."

"What big words for such a little girl!" she says, making her eyes big. "Do you want me to call the Missing Children's desk?"

"Nah," I say, trying to sound nonchalant. "She'll be here." But my voice is squeaky.

"OK, sweetie, but if there's a problem you just call me. Now, why don't you sit on this nice big couch?"

She pats me on the head. I roll my eyes and try to mumble thanks, the way I've been raised to.

Hurry up forcrissake, I think, you want a screaming six-year-old on your hands?

I crawl up to the fake leather couch and dangle my little legs over the edge. I almost hypnotize myself watching my white anklets, my little red Mary Janes, kick back and forth, back and forth.

"You must be Robin."

I'm sucking my thumb, half asleep on the huge couch. I look up at his big face, wipe the drool from my mouth and brush my hand against the paper name tag pinned on my little girl overcoat: "My name is Robin Daley. I don't know where I am."

I nod.

"Hi, Robin. I was sent to pick you up."

He puts his huge hand out to me as if to take my little one in his. I thrust my right hand out to him and shake as sturdily as I can. He grins like I'm just too adorable for words.

"What manners!" he says like he's Jimmy Stewart talking to the next Shirley Temple.

"Forcrissake, it took you long enough," I snap, stretching up to him. "Where is she?"

"She couldn't make it today . . . well, actually she never gets to airports anymore, so she sent me."

"Oh," I growl.

Mom had never flown after that one trip, but she always, *always* came to see me off when I went away, whether it was for a week at summer camp, a weekend meet for high school or even a visit to Dad. She'd stand there at the exit gate, sniffing and waving till the plane was gone. And when I got back, I'd see her the minute they let us near the door, waving at me frantically, her huge awful black plastic purse sliding down her arm. To be honest, I'd been embarrassed when she screeched, "There's my baby!! There's my little angel!" and grabbed me like I was a six-year-old who'd just returned from concentration camp. At least I wouldn't have to worry about that anymore.

Her driver squats down on his knees and looks at me eye to eye. "I know you've been taught not to talk to strangers, but I'm your friend."

"Cut the crap, buddy," I snarl, "just offer me a piece of candy and I'll get in your car with you. Let's get the hell outta this joint."

I jump off the plastic couch and look behind him into the lobby. Maybe it's that I no longer recognize it from knee's eye view, but I think it's more than that. I think this is a new airport I've never been to before.

I look behind him again.

"You need to go to the little girls' room?" he asks quietly. "It's a pretty long drive."

"What I need is another goddamned bourbon," I retort.

He laughs and ruffles up my hair. "I think you need a nap," he says in his Mr. Rogers voice.

He reaches his big hand down to me, and, reluctantly, I stretch mine up to him. My little frilly pink skirt and petticoats creak when I walk.

"I feel scratchy," I whine involuntarily. "I wanna go home."

The car is flashy, new, a ritzy Italian sports model, more suave than anything I saw in Europe. He bundles me up in a soft flannel blanket in the seat next to him.

"Try and take a nap, Robbie," he says sweetly.

"Nobody calls me that, shitface," I spit. Then my lower lip

is quivering. "I wanna go home." I stick my thumb in my mouth.

I try to stay awake and see the new buildings that have sprung up in my absence. The airport seems so strange and new, but they'd built it just before I left. But I'm so sleepy and my head feels heavy. He pats me on the head. I'm out before he even starts the engine.

The dream I'm having is of home. It's the apartment in Woodland Park and Shirley, the woman from 15B, is knocking on our door asking if we can hide Bobby Lee because Willy is coming around and she expects the worst. Mom says we can and then Bobby Lee is there and so is Shirley, and Shirley is making those silk roses she makes at the factory and Bobby Lee is riding Willy's pickup in the hall and he and Tim are playing catch. I'm under the counter because the whole apartment has become filled with the awful scent of fake roses and I can't get to my bed. I think my mother lifts me up. I think she tries to pull me from the counter. I think she carries me, my sleep-drugged body heavy as a child. She holds me next to her. I think she shakes me in my bed. I think she whispers, "Robin, Robin. . ."

Then it is my mother waking me up. I open my eyes and I think my mom has rescued me from another nightmare, but once I get a good look at her, I'm not so sure.

"Robin Daley, Robin Daley. . ."

She's leaning over me to give me a hug like she did when I was in grade school when she woke me up for school, only instead of saying, "Wake up, angel," she's saying, "Welcome,

Robin Daley." And instead of smelling like coffee and milk and the honey buns she's just put in the toaster oven, she smells like flowery perfume. And instead of hugging me, she puts her hands firmly on my shoulders.

I can't manage to get out a "hello, Mom" or even a "good morning." I try not to worry too much, attributing it to jet lag.

Mom is dressed like I've never seen her before. She's slim and tan and she's had a facelift. She's wearing a white silk toga that brings out her sunlamp color even more. Her gray hair has all been moved to one place — a dashing streak. She's wearing those little strapped sandals like you see the models wear in travel brochures of the Mediterranean. And over her eyes, a pair of shiny black, reflecting sunglasses.

I close my eyes and tighten my grip on her, trying to feel the comfortable old shape I remember.

I lean to her, and whisper "Mom" into her clothes.

Then she's holding me. I try to hold her tighter. I don't want to let her go.

"Mom," I can barely croak.

She loosens her grip and tells me, "There, there," the way I've never heard anyone say in real life, only seen in those grade-B sentimental movies we used to laugh at at the matinees.

"There, there," she says again, and pulls away from me.

She sits at the end of my bed, her hands across her lap. The wall behind her seems to stretch so far. The room is bigger than it was.

I rub what I hope is sleep from my eyes, and scan the walls. My high school pennant is gone, and all my posters.

"Mom?"

The design trophy I got in UTA isn't on top of the dresser. The dresser's gone.

"Mom?"

The lamp beside my bed is not the one I made in Girl Scouts, but a sleek, black techno model.

"Mom?"

But she's still not answering me.

I pull the covers over me tighter. It's not the flannel cowboy blanket I used to have, but a down comforter, maroon with slate gray trim.

"Where are we, Mom?" I can't tell if I whisper or shout. I close my eyes and hope I'll hear her whisper back, over the front seat of the car, "I'm not sure, hon, but we should be there soon."

But that's not it. No. She whisks me out to a balcony outside my bedroom window. I look down to see the parking lot with the speed bumps, the dumpsters and wrecked cars where Bobby Lee and Tim and me and everyone used to hang out. Instead, there's a panorama of the mountains. They stretch out everywhere. The exterior of the house is pink marble and there's vines growing over the garden walls that extend as far as I can see. Below me is a court-yard with statues of little naked Roman-looking boys and girls. In the pond in the garden, a little boy statue pees into a fish's mouth.

I turn around and ask my mother, "Where are we?" The sun behind her blinds me and I only see her in a darkened silhouette, her thin silk toga billowing behind her in a wind that I can't feel, the harsh sun glinting off her dark sunglasses.

"Where are we going?" My mouth moves, but I can't make a sound. It's like when you've been shouting and shouting and shouting in a nightmare and you think you've been awake, but it's all been in your sleep and then you finally shout aloud—"Mom?"

But when she looks at me, it's like she doesn't hear me shout at all. Her face is careful, quiet, poised.

"Where are we, Mom?" I ask. "Where is this place?"

The line that she delivers is graceful and cool. Her voice is square and stiff.

"Consider this your home now, Robin. You are most welcome here. And call me Lucia."

But I had fantasized the Great Return.

She meets me at the airport and almost doesn't recognize me. I've changed so much; I've grown so "continental." I've replaced my beat-up, hand-me-down flight jacket with a slate gray, fine leather coat, exquisitely tailored to bring out the sharp lines of my shoulders, my perfect tiny hips. My windswept hair is blown back from my face. My jaw is firm. My cheeks are thin.

I'm moving quickly through the crowd, flinging over my shoulder my well-worn, trusty brown leather bag (the one that exudes an air of sophisticated worldliness). My hands are tan. I wear two gold rings which obviously mean something, but something so private and intimate I'll never tell. I breeze through the crowd, towering over the John and Jane Q. Publics ogling for their American Tourister sets. But when I walk through them, they start to ogle me.

But I can't decide what happens next. I don't know if it's

her, the way I left her, sweet and plump and dumpy, her big purse falling down her arm, screeching, "There's my baby!!"

Or if she's someone else.

And then, it goes like this:

I come in through the door from the plane looking distracted. I've been thinking important, passionate, unsayable Great Things. (Also, profound.) About what I've left behind in Italy, about being a Woman Without a Country, about being a world-wide and world-weary traveler, etc.

I'm taller than everyone else in the crowd. I see her first. Her back is to me. I close my eyes and will her to turn around. When I open my eyes, she's looking at me. I hold her with my eyes. I think a hushed "hello," but don't say anything.

I smile my special hearty smile, the one I've worked on so long to perfect, when my left cheek gets those wonderful lines in it. I step toward her. She reaches her right hand for me to shake. I take it in both of mine, lean to her, and kiss her cheek. Her eyelashes blink against my skin. She smells my subtle perfume.

"It's good to see you," I whisper suggestively, then lean away from her. I smile again.

"You've changed," she whispers, breathlessly.

I pat her hand with both of mine.

"Well, it's been a while," I say. "Everybody changes."

She looks down at herself and laughs. "Well, some more than others."

"So," I announce crisply, "I've got some bags around here somewhere."

She follows me to the baggage claim. I can feel her looking

at my back—the sheen of Spanish leather and weave of English wool, the brisk cut of my sharp Italian boots.

I watch the luggage then dip gracefully for my Italian designer bags. When I pull them off, she runs her hands over the soft, strong leather, the tough brass rings.

She looks up at me, admiringly.

I talk to the depths of her deep blue eyes when I tell her, "Some of us didn't need to change so much."

I pause dramatically. "I went away so I could come back."

That's when she nods, her mouth just slightly open, when I see the white rims of her perfect teeth.

And though there're people everywhere, and though my voice is low, we don't hear anything but when I say, *"I'm back."*

She leans to me. I feel her breath, her mouth—she opens up her perfect mouth and whispers—finally she tells me—yes—finally her mouth—she tells me—yes—finally she tells me—

"But where are we, Mom?" I whine.

"We've got to keep that secret," Mother answers, interrupting me. "We can't have all my public trying to haunt me."

"I'm not your public."

Her eyes snap, stopping me.

"I just want to know where we live."

"We're on location," Momma says, then mumbles something I don't hear.

I try to place the mountains and the air. I try hard to remember: have I ever seen this sky before?

***

I try to sleep. It feels like it's been years. I sleep for days.

I stumble through her house, the flights of twisty stairs, and corridors, the giant cluttered rooms. I'm about to give myself up for lost—*where am I*—when I find the kitchen. I'm starved. I start to heat up a frozen honey bun for breakfast when, suddenly a crew of chefs, big white hats and all, are whipping up omelettes for sixteen. I shuffle out of their way, though they barely notice me. They're speaking Italian. I peek out the window and see my mother on the terrace, holding court. A maid pours from a silver tea set. My mother drinks her mineral water from a champagne glass. She tells her listeners anecdotes about Life Behind the Scenes. I watch her arms, her billowing sleeves.

Her guests are all completely gorgeous. I stand by the sink eating my Morton's frozen breakfast bun and watch them pick at their asparagus omelettes with walnut sauce, their tangerine juice fresh squeezed by the faithful gardener, their hot, homemade croissants. They titter at my mother's jokes. I watch my mother's eyes, though I have difficulty seeing them through her black sunglasses.

My mother lives with strangers in her home. They truly are my mom's adoring public. They work for her. They deal with the rest of her wild, unruly fans. They send out her promotion kits. They answer fan mail. They take out the trash. They oooh and aaah at her latest clothes. They preen her pets. They listen to her stories and they laugh. They tell her they will never leave.

There're hundreds of them, thousands, I can't count.

I try to meet them, but I can't. They change from day to

day, they come and leave. They're always moving. New ones take their places, almost similar, but not one of them stays. Does Mother know?

I ask my mother who they are: amusing people, new-found confidantes, young talent, struggling stars ("Like myself in a former life," she laughs). They come and go.

"We're one big, happy family," Momma says. And she believes it.

Q: *Was Robin shocked to see her mother?*
A: Shocked would be putting it mildly. If the truth be known, she was aghast. She thought her mother looked like a prostitute and looked like she was living like a prostitute.

Q: *What would Robin have liked the reunion to have been like?*
A: She would have liked her mother to have driven up to the airport in Dallas in her shitty old beat-up Ford and taken Robin back home to their old apartment so they could eat a simple meal together, say a frozen pizza, while the two of them talked about what they'd done for the past few years. She would have liked for her mother to tell her how proud she (her mother) was of her (Robin), and her work. And she would have liked her mother to report that she (Mrs. Daley) had found a nice little job at the library or at the school administration building and was working with nice people, etc. Then asked Robin further about her interesting and esoteric and fascinating work in domestic architecture.

Q: *What did Robin hate most about her mother when she returned to her mother's home?*

A: The fact that everyone called her mother "Lucia," and that she (Mrs. Daley) referred to herself, in fact, as "Lucia."

Q: *What did Robin secretly want to do all the time?*

A: Call her mother Mom in front of everyone all the time and have them start calling her Betty Daley.

Q: *Did Robin think much about her brother Timothy at this time?*

A: Frankly, no. Only when she really needed someone. But she did make a case for it when she wanted to make her mother feel bad that she (Mrs. Daley) didn't think about him enough.

Q: *What became Robin's favorite literature to think about during this difficult time?*

A: *Dr. Jekyll and Mr. Hyde, Pygmalion,* the myth of Narcissus, *The Picture of Dorian Gray,* her own great exposé, possibly through a series of interviews in national glossies, which would expose her mother for the hypocritical shithead she really was.

Q: *What became, in fact, the literature that Robin actually read during this time?*

A: *Screen, The Hollywood Reporter, Star, Rona Barrett's Gossip Column, Daily Variety, Movie Digest,* etc.

Q: *What excuse did Robin offer for reading the very trash she claimed to despise?*

A: It was always lying around the place.

Q: *What was the first thing Robin thought about every morning?*

A: Her mother.

Q: *What was the last thing Robin thought about before she went to sleep each night?*

A: Her mother.

Q: *What was the thing that occupied the greatest portion of Robin's thought, both conscious and subconscious?*

A: Her mother.

Q: *Can you be more specific?*

A: How much she hated her mother, what a hypocrite her mother was, what a shithead her mother was, how her mother used to be so open and sincere and how now she was a shithead, how she hated the fact that the thing her mother valued most about herself was her "image" (to quote her mother), how she wished her mother were poor and dumpy and unadored (not that she had ever been those things before, mind you), and then maybe she'd remember who her real friends were. How she truly adored her mother, how she thought her mother had shitty taste in clothes, gaudy taste in housewares, abominable taste in homes, how she spent money in a manner unfitting to a human being, how she (Robin) was the only one in the world that really, truly knew her mother, how she hated and disrespected her mother's legion of companions, how she wondered if her mother would ever think of her again if she (Robin) left her (her mother) again, even if she *really* left, for good, especially after delivering the speech or some variation of the speech she often fantasized giving her. Her incredible remorse whenever she did actually get mad at or confront her mother or talk about her behind her back, even think about her behind her back, true through many of the things were that she (Robin) said and thought. The incredible ambiguity of her feelings, thoughts and otherwise about her mother.

Q: *What exactly was this speech that Robin fantasized giving her mother?*

A: There were many, many versions.

Dear Tim,

Where are you? I asked Mom about you but she won't tell me. I'm sending copies of this letter to all the schools we thought of sending you to. I hope I find you. I hope we can get back together.

But I'm not much better myself. I don't know where I am either. I'm at Mom's new place, but she moved while I was gone and I don't know where we are. I guess I shouldn't be surprised, but she's changed so much, Tim. She's not her old self anymore. You must have seen it happen, you poor thing. You saw our Mom become a star overnight.

Write to me, Tim. We've got to try to find each other. I'm sure you can get ahold of me via her studio. I hope you can get through. Where are you? Write me. I swear, I'll come back to you.

XX,
Robin

She touts me as a famous architect. I don't correct her. She tells them I've done projects all around the world: in Turkey and in Thailand, and in France, Bombay, New Zealand. In places I have never heard of. Italy.

"Tell us about Italy, Robin," my mother says. She spreads her fine arms in a wide, inclusive gesture. "I've never been to Italy." This lie's for them. She smiles as if she really is as innocent as they want her to be. She knows that I won't challenge her in front of them.

And though I'm already tired of my ragged slides, my suggestive, half-completed stories of the other, richer life I led, my travel anecdotes, I want her to be proud of me. I let her bring me out and plug me in.

I show for her, her followers, the slides of all my journeys. I show them little gems, quaint homes and restaurants, white dusty villas, tiny inns still undiscovered by the average tourist. I tell tales about the people that I met on trains, in small hotels. They know I make friends easily with strangers.

"That's her, that's Robin," Momma says. She points to me, my image on the wall, where I stand by famous buildings, sit beneath striped umbrellas with a drink. I wave and smile from miles and years away. I wear the sleek Italian jacket that I thought I'd only dreamt about. "That's her," my mother tells them. "She's on tour." I think she's trying to show she's proud of me, the faraway exciting life I led. But she never talks to me direct.

Night after night, I stand in the back of her giant movie room filled with her hordes of fans, and keep my thumb pressed on the slide machine. I watch my mother's outline in the silver dark, the glitter of her rings when she catches a shaft of light. Sometimes I'll see her arm raised up in front of the image I project. And truly, I must admit, I like the way I look on screen.

My face is tan. I smile with confidence. I almost wouldn't recognize me. What was I thinking when they took this photograph? Perhaps I was genuinely happy. But perhaps I was looking forward to happiness, was looking, even then, when this was shot, into the camera lens for her, to telling her my stories when I came back.

But each new time I tell it, it gets dull. Soon I stand unnoticed in the dark. The me she sees is on the screen. The me that stands here, finger on the slide box, could be anyone. I stumble through my stories, my voice shaky and scared, not anything like the voice you'd expect from the brisk confident traveler I project. In fact, I feel I could be telling someone else's travels. And anybody could be reading this script.

So later, in my room when I'm alone, my mother comes to me. She startles me in the middle of the night. I hear her standing outside my bedroom door calling out my name in a stage whisper, "Robin! Robin!" She sneaks to me and holds me, whispers closely, intimately, "Oh, Robin dear, you've got to change the script."

I pull away from her and whisper back, "But that's not the way it happened, Mom."

"That doesn't matter," Momma says. "Make it dramatic, gorgeous. Put some life in it."

I shrug, both tired and envious of my former life. "Besides," I sigh, "they wouldn't do things like that in Rome. You know that."

"How would I know that? I've never been to Italy."

"Come on, Mom."

"I've never been to Italy."

"Mom," I sigh again, rubbing my tired eyes, "I won't tell you what to say to them, but you don't need to lie to me. You've been to Italy. You went there years ago with me and Tim to visit D—"

"I have not been to Italy," she says deliberately.

I look at her dark sunglasses and realize she means it.

"Change the script," she whispers. "You've got to keep your audience. Make it exotic, faraway."

"Faraway from *where*?" I snap. "You won't even tell me where we are!"

"We're on location," Momma says. "Just do it." Her eyes dart around my room. "Well, I . . . here—I'll help. I'll do it." She gathers up my slides and notes and rushes from my room.

I know my mother will do anything to keep her adoring public. She tells me, if you don't know where you are, you'll never leave.

Soon, she's made me put away my beat-up flight jacket, and is dressing me in the native dress of countries I have visited. She marches me up to the screen and stands me next to my projected image. I wear the native garb she talks about. I sing authentic-sounding ethnic songs that she's made up. In broken English and the accent of the "old country" I tell the "folk tales" mother has created. I'm her prop. She tells them anecdotes of things that never happened. They believe her.

In secret, Momma meets me in my room. Between ourselves, we make a secret pact. We tell ourselves it isn't bad, our rearranging truth and myth. We only make it pretty for her loyal, loving fans. We want to make them happy. And, we want to make them stay.

My mother's live-in transient fan club grows. She wants to keep them all: "I want to make them feel like they can stay. We need more room."

We walk her house together and she whispers to me, soft and intimate. I can feel her breath, her body, leaning to me saying, "Robin, Robin, this is what I want.

"I want this hall to look like this, this stair to look like this, I want these walls to meet like this, this ceiling painted thus. I want the roof and the exterior, the pipes and window-panes. I want the lamps, and library, the lawn. I want a room for everyone. I want the door and banisters. I want the porcelain and trim. I want the study and the den, the porch. I want the hallways and the floor. I want the windows, lights. I want the mantelpiece. I want it here. I want a —"

But then she wants a word that she's forgotten.

Thus my mother hires me to restore her stately home.

My mother says, "You seem to understand, almost intuitively, just what I want. Just how I want things done. I don't know what the connection is, but sometimes when we look at the same thing, like that archway in the foyer, we just look at it and smile at one another, knowing we're thinking the same thing. I don't know how you do it. You draw it just like I thought it."

I don't know if my mother's teasing me. Of course we think alike, and see this house alike. We share each other's memory and blood.

We're walking through the main hall of the second floor and I'm talking about paint and wallpaper. We're standing next to this huge old painting, a romantic portrait of two old fogies. The woman in the portrait has pink cheeks. The man is studiously tan and rugged, and sports a rakish beret. They both look like they're sixty. In the background, true to allegorical portraiture, is a fuzzy, fake acropolis. And the Colosseum. It looks really dumb.

I laugh. "Who the hell are these two old farts? Did they used to own this joint?" Half of me is joking, and the other half is hoping I'll catch Mom off guard, and she'll admit to me something about this place. I still do not know where we are, or how she found it here.

But all she does is giggle too.

"Well," I sigh, "it's gotta go." I lift the painting off the wall. "Just look how that's faded." I tap the wallpaper that stayed dark behind the frame.

"Hey, listen to that." I knock again. "It's hollow."

"What?" My mother asks. Her voice is tight.

I tap the wall again. "I think there's something back there."

She takes my arm and pulls me along with her. "Listen. I don't want to get too out of hand with this renovation stuff. God knows we could knock the whole thing down. Who knows how they built it in the first place."

"Who, Mom? Who'd you buy this from? Whose house was this?"

"Just keep with the cosmetic stuff," she orders me. "Just keep with what you see."

"You won't even tell me where we are," I press.

"We're on location—"

She won't look at me.

"Whose house was this?" I ask. "Where are we?"

She spins away from me and starts briskly down the hall.

"But I—" I shout.

She stops.

I speak as slow and careful as I can, as logical as if I told the truth. "But I need to know where we are so I can use indigenous materials, so it'll fit, so that. . ." But I even sound limp to me.

"You're only here because you've been hired to do a job," she says, still facing away from me. "No other reason."

I nod. We're silent.

Then slowly, she turns back. I look down the hall at her shiny black glasses.

"This is *my house*."

I nod so she can see me.

And it is, I remind myself. This is my mother's home.

I lean the portrait against the wall. She laughs as if nothing has happened.

"Hey look at this."

I walk toward her. As gently, as if she's being tender, Momma whispers, "Can you change this corridor? I want the trim to shine. I want the grandstand and the lawn. I want it new." She sounds like she's reciting something she's rehearsed for years.

"Mom—" I start to answer. But she shudders.

She pushes me into a tiny room off the hallway. It's a small room, hardly bigger than a closet, and dustless, airless, gray. She looks behind her, left and right, furtive.

When she's sure no one's seen or heard us, she steps in

behind me. She wrings her hands and whispers quick: "Don't call me that."

My mouth is open wide.

She swallows, leans her head to the closed door, and listens to make sure there's no one in the hall.

"I'm not that," she whispers.

"Not what?" I whisper too.

"I'm not your mother."

"What?"

"I'm not your mother."

I look at her and think she's trying to play a joke, to test us both. I break into a smile and reach to her. Suddenly she looks so tiny and fragile, and I know, I *know* she just wants me to tell her that I will always be her daughter, that no matter what kind of image she has to sell her public, I will remain true, that I will never leave her.

"Look," I tell her sweetly, "you don't have to tell me you're not my mom."

"I'm not."

I think, beneath her sunglasses, she looks at me. I put my hands on her shoulders and feel her skin beneath her clothes, my hands. I look into her sunglasses and try to see her deep blue angel eyes.

I know, I *know* she sees herself in me. I whisper gently, "Mom."

"I never had a daughter," Momma says, each word deliberate. She shifts underneath my hands. Her face is turned to me, but she's not looking at me. Her eyes dart beneath the lenses.

"Mom," I tighten my grip on her shoulders, "I'm your daughter. I was born in —"

"I never married." She takes a firm step back from me. My hands are empty.

"You did, Mom." I step toward her. "You married my father—"

"I never married him." Her voice is flat and loud. "I never married anyone."

"What about Tim? You—"

"I never had a son."

She sounds like she's reciting lines. "I am nobody's mother, no one's wife."

I stare at her, her graceful neck, her fine hands, the manners that she's learned in Hollywood. The line of her skin in the gray, nonlight of this tiny room, her eyes that dart around, beyond me into nothing.

"I did it all alone. I am my own. I represent—"

I interrupt, but slowly, like I'm helping her. I say, "OK, Mom, OK." I swallow like a cop coaxing a teenager from the roof. "I agree with you that nobody should define themselves by the way they are to other people. And I think it's fine the studio helped you with that image. You are your own person, Lucia. I'm not saying that being my mom is all you are, but . . ." I strain to try to remember all the pabulum she read in those self-help books before she finally went back to school. "But—"

"I'm not your mother," her voice declares, as if she hasn't heard me. "No daughter of mine would ever—" She stops and gulps. "No son of mine—" She gasps. "I would never marry anyone who'd—" She chokes.

"Who'd what, Mom?"

Her mouth moves, but she isn't talking out loud anymore.

I watch her mouth move like a movie with the sound track off. I try to read her lips. I can't.

But sometimes from the corner of my eye, I see her watching me, from the corner of her eye. I think I see her recognize a gesture, or the way I turn my head. I think she sees it in my eyes, the way I hold my drink, my hands.

But she won't tell me anything. She turns her head.

"I'll do what I can, Ma'am," I say, professional, the architect she's hired. My hard hat makes a rustic shadow on my face. "But we got a lotta kinks to work out, lady."

I send my crew through the house. They mingle with her fans. We redo plumbing, wiring. We hire black-dressed chimney sweeps to empty out the flues. We prune.

But some of this, I want to do myself. Too many walls sound hollow and the roof's too high above the ceiling. Things rattle when I tap them. There must be keys to unlock all the sealed doors.

I ask my crew of locals what they know about the house, or where they live. My mother must have gotten to them first, for they don't answer.

I feel like I'm working in the dark. Without a blueprint or a plan, my mother tells me, "Cover this, and knock out that. New trim. New paint, new fixtures."

She wants to make it like it's all brand-new.

I do. And then, the house is done.

So Momma throws a party. The place is packed: producers and directors, rising young stars and starlets, people with tons of bucks and people who want to meet the people with tons of bucks. I'm standing near the fireplace in the living room nursing a bottle of bourbon in one-shot installments. I lean against the mantelpiece trying to look like I'm waiting for my special someone to return with our hors d'oeuvres, rather than standing around wishing I wasn't there at all.

Then Mom breezes into the mom followed by half a dozen hangers-on. I recognize some of them from the press and a few almost regular house groupies. As usual, she's holding court. She's telling an anecdote and they're all on the edge of their drinks waiting to clap the loudest, laugh the quickest or take her gracious hand and kiss it first. I'm wearing black beneath my tight-zipped flight jacket and making history of a fifth of whiskey. They titter at her anecdotes then make ever such urbane small talk afterward. "Oh, Lucia, tell us more about this marvelous place you've found." They're all begging for a tidbit they can take back to their breathless waiting underlings, a casual familiar story: "Oh, I was chatting with Lucia Holmes at her lovely housewarming. . ."

I glare at them through the brittle edge of drink and watch their gestures; practiced, perfect, waiting for the stage. I watch the way they hold their glasses, cigarettes, the way they casually brush her arm. She's telling them this story:

". . . Imagine my surprise when I tapped the wall behind this wonderful old portrait of that delightful old couple, and found it was hollow. Isn't it just fascinating what those people built back then." She lifts her face, her smile, radiant, gathers up her skirts, and sails across the room. They scuttle behind her like penguins vying for position.

Does she see me watching her? Does she know I've heard her tell a tale from which I've been removed?

I know my mother has no idea how they built things "back then," or even when "back then" was. The crowd behind her nods in unison. "Yes, fascinating, Lucia, a wonderful find." I nurse my sweaty bourbon and try to catch her eye. I wonder if she'll keep me on now that my job is finished.

The night goes on forever. My vision starts to blur and all my mother's followers begin to look alike. I don't talk to anyone, but no one seems to notice I'm alone.

So I get drunk.

I sway up to the second floor and drop myself inside her bedroom door. I doze to the sound of her party below, the rumbling of the extras. I hear through the cotton blur of my whiskey-sleep, the camera's whirr, the swish and thump of sets being replaced. I huddle in the dark.

Then—I don't know when this is—I hear her dresses rustling up the stairs. I shut my eyes tight and hug my arms around my aching head.

I'm going to catch her.

I hear my mother's titter down the hall. She's talking to herself, but low, like she's afraid there's someone else to hear. I hear her open the door behind me and flick on the overhead light.

"Oh, that light's so bright," I moan, and squint away from the swaying chandelier.

My mother gasps and slams the door closed behind her.

Head on the floor, I watch her black high heels angle over to me, each tiny step a jab against the floor.

"You're—you're *drunk*," her voice shoots down to me.

"You're disgusting. Just like yo—" Then she catches herself and grabs her breath.

"Like who?" I press, my garbled voice.

I try to focus on my mother's face. Her mouth is tight, but moving underneath the shadow of her sunglasses.

"Like *who*?" I insist. But already my eyes are closing and I know she'll outlast me again. "Who?" I try to ask again, but my voice is trapped on the spit in my throat.

I think I hear her exhale with relief. She doesn't answer me.

And though this is the first time that she's ever seen me drunk, she knows exactly what to do: to hold my head over the john, to feed me black coffee and walk me out in the air. She holds my sagging, heaving shoulders and sits with me, stiff and waiting. I start to whine an apology, but I don't.

There's something about the angle of her face, the way her head is bowed away from me that looks familiar. And I can tell it feels familiar to her too.

I put my hands on the side of my head and moan. I feel my mother look at me. I hear her voice:

"There's just one way to beat them leaving you," she says.

"What are you talking about?"

Again, she doesn't answer me. I think I sleep. I think she carries me. I think she holds my head.

"Where are you going?" I shout above the chorus.

They're carrying her luggage out. I pour myself a bourbon and look for her. They're all dressed up, her men, her handsome, rugged rising stars, in those smart little tuxedos and top hats the dancers wear in the 1930s musicals. They're skittering around singing Broadway songs and packing her beautiful Italian bags into the limos. I slouch by the big front door and clutch my bourbon when I see my mother swing down the wide open staircase in her white fur. She carries a little white poodle on her arm. Her sunglasses are black and hard and shiny.

"Where are you going?" I yell up to her as she glides down the staircase.

"We're shooting in New York," my mother says. "We won't be gone more than a few weeks. You'll be a darling and watch the house for us while we're away, mmm?" she says without stopping to hear my answer. She's out the door. I fumble along behind her.

"How are you getting there?" I hope she'll slip and tell me, "Oh, we're taking 29 north," or "We're catching the Crescent in Philly," and I'll get some idea where we are. But she's quicker than me. "The car, my dear, the car."

She snaps her fingers and two of her beautiful boys come sweep up the tail of her coat and hold it while she steps into the limo that's pulled up to her. Her poodle growls at me over her shoulder and she melts into the car. One of her boys closes the door behind her. I watch her silhouette in the back seat, behind the square of the shiny black car window. She sinks back into her seat and I can't see her.

I watch her caravan of limos fill. Her furs and hats, her followers, their hampers of pâté and champagne, the lockers full of costumes. Her boys all move like Fred Astaire. There're hundreds of them. I watch their spats, their bowties and cravats, their gorgeous coats and tails. I hear corks pop in every car but Mom's. I wave them off and watch the tail of shiny black ease down the mountain like a snake.

She leaves me in her house alone.

My feet are loud and heavy on the marble floors. I picture Momma walking through these halls, the open sleeves of her dark nightgown billowing. I see her in the mirror in the entryway, her face reflected on the long dining room table, the window looking out back to the mountains.

I go to Mother's room and look at what she lives with. I'm jealous of the radiator, the drip of paint on the underside of the window ledge. These things live with her almost every day. When my mother gazes out the window, takes her sunglasses from her face, puts the earpiece in her mouth and chews unconsciously, they see all that. I stand in her room and stare.

That night I sleep in Mother's bed.

I wake up, startled from my sleep. I think I've heard a sound. I reach for the bedside lamp and flick it on. It's dead. I lie there for a few seconds hoping my eyes will adjust. When I start for the door to switch on the overhead lights, I trip on something. I move aside, then take another step and bump into something else. I squint in the ungiving dark and run my hands over what blocks my way. It feels like a chair. I touch the knobby surface — corduroy. I run my suddenly wet palms against it softly. My fingers trace the edges of the back, the tucks of cloth between the back and arms. I stretch my hands taut to push the cloth with a pressure equal to its own. I turn my palm around and feel the texture give against my skin. My skin tingles, as if I've never touched anything before. My fingers separate and find small ridges, like folds of skin, the untouched secret corners that have never been exposed. My finger finds the seam between the corduroy and canvas. I stroke the thread, then run my flat palm in between the cushion and the arms. I tuck my fingertips into the crevices behind the bottom cushion as if I'm looking for a lost pen or an earring. My hand leaves moisture when I pull it out.

This chair was not in this room when I went to bed.

I squat on the ground, sucking in my frightened breath, and put my face against the soft brushed cloth. Then I crawl up into the chair and sink. I know what I've been touching. I close my eyes.

How did this get into her room?

Like a blind woman, I stumble, trying to remember where our furniture used to be. I walk slowly as the floor plan recurs to me. I stalk the hall down to where our living room was.

I run my shaking hands along the rough-painted wall, and take the three steps I remember to the big old couch in Monterey. I walk along behind it, rubbing my hand along the stiff thread that springs out of it. I turn to find, behind me, almost eye level now, the door knobs to the liquor cabinet in Kansas City. I open the cabinet with a creak and reach inside. I run my skin on the different shapes of bottles, glasses, ashtrays. I close the cabinet and follow my desperate hands along the wall — the photographs we took, in frames, the tape beside the pencil lines when we marked off our height, his Million Miler Award. I veer into the kitchen in Arlington; the refrigerator where Mom stood when she packed Tim's and my lunches, the barstool where we sat when she told me he'd lost his job. And here is Timmy's stool. Then I can smell breakfast, the frozen honey buns, her instant cup of coffee. This is the counter where we ate in Milton, the table where we threw our coats. This is the table where we ate, the corner where we had the tree in Jacksonville. My eyes, still shocked, and unadjusted, do not see. I grope. My hands try hard, remembering.

I stand as quiet as I can and hold my breath. I squint and barely see, outlined in gray, in one small tiny filament of light, the ghostly outlines of my family's rooms. On top of one another, the images shift for space, our furniture, possessions; what we lost.

I don't know how I find my room again. I wake up in my own bed when the morning mountain light cuts into me. It's bright and brilliant, hopping off the furniture I see too clearly.

I jolt from bed and run throughout my movie-actress mother's mansion. I look for rooms that I remember, though I do not know from when.

Then, on the carpet in the first-floor parlor, there's a dent. It could have been my family's couch; the shadow on the wall, his liquor cabinet.

Then Momma's home. It feels like it's been years.

I hear my mother's caravan of limos, smooth, unzipping up the mountainside. I climb the third-floor balcony and watch them mount the road, a shiny snake that separates and fuses back. I know Mom is in the first car, sipping her mineral water, reading her *Hollywood Reporter* through her sunglasses. I can almost hear her say, wishing someone could overhear her perfect accent, "Oh, it is lovely to be back in my country hideaway, so far from the horrid workaday world." I can almost see her in her shiny Rolls — she never flies — her head held high in the back seat behind her chauffeur. "I don't want them gawking at me," she'd say in her haughty voice. But she'd be watching, from behind her dark sunglasses, through the tinted window of the car, out at the world to see who's looking for her, hoping she'll inspire them to say, "Oh there goes Lucia Holmes, that mysterious, gracious star."

I'm standing at the top of her grand staircase when she appears at the open door. The sun is brilliant, bright and clean behind her. It shoots off her full white fur coat, the rims of her sunglasses, surrounding her. I hear her swishing up the stairs, her feet across the marble. I can't see her face.

But I can tell that she looks up to me.

The closer she gets to me, I see her face like an image rising out of a polaroid picture.

"How'd it go?" I ask her sunglasses, nonchalant as I can.

"Oh, it was terrific," she says with a tired sigh. "But it's time for me to be home."

I feel my skin stand up. She steps toward me.

"Where is everyone?" None of her pretty boys has come into the house. I don't hear them unpacking cars, or tapping across the drive in their traveling George M. Cohan tap-shoes, tossing bags to the tune of a Broadway song.

"Oh," she waves, as if she can wave them away, "they're showing some photographers around the grounds. They'll be here soon. But Robin, something happened while I was gone. I've been thinking. I want to talk with you."

I hold my breath. My skin is cold. She steps right next to me. I think, beneath her sunglasses, she blinks.

She puts her arm around me. It feels like years.

I make a point not to look at her, but concentrate on the old feeling of her warm, big floppy arm on me. I know that if I look at her direct, her touch will change.

I bring her to my room.

I light a fire.

Sometimes it's been so long since there's been anything, I almost stop. I almost think, "I'm wrong, it's just my longing thinking we are kin." That's when my wanting changes shape, from pointed, sharp, direct, and so near to the surface and the almost-said, into the soft, almost unsayable and numb. Just when I almost have forgotten, she'll give something—a look, a touch, the brush of her hand on my skin, her cool palm on my forehead. Or a word. And it will stay with me, inhere, a burn as clean and hot as snow after a steaming bath. That's when I'll let myself think once again, despite her innocent denials, we are blood. But I keep this secret in myself. I won't acknowledge it to her, just hope that she remembers deeper than her hard will to forget.

I light a fire.

I pour her a mineral water and an orange soda for me.

Mom and I are in my room. She smiles and brings the glass to her mouth. I watch the smoky vapor rise. Her neck moves when she opens her throat to drink.

When I open my mouth, I feel the skin of my lips slip apart. I take my tongue from my teeth and pull the soda into my throat.

My mother looks down at her glass, the tiny bubbles hopping on the surface. She runs her finger on the gold rim of the glass. It hums. I think she looks at me from behind her sunglasses.

She turns away and looks out the western window. I see her shoulders rise when she takes a deep, deep breath of air.

Her back is to me. She lifts her hands to her face, and takes her glasses off.

I open my mouth.

I hear her sigh.

I want to call her "Mom." I start to say —

This afternoon is made of gold. This day's a certain shade of gold, this certain afternoon. This certain angle is a meeting point, a certain point when gold meets gold and shadows turn to lines. Each thing in my bedroom brings something back. It resonates. Her hands are on the glass. Her skin is luminous. My mother's hair has caught the light. The glass glows. The sharp curve down my mother's neck is radiant. The line of sun behind her, her ear, her jaw, her chin, the wrinkles on my mother's neck, her almost seen, uncovered eyes —

I almost say —

But then she stands. The light shatters when she walks to the door. I watch the sun drip off her back. She raises her arm, her back still to me, and puts her glasses back on. She turns to me.

"We're going to do a retrospective of my career on TV. I'll have you do the research. We can keep you on here for a while."

Suddenly the light is in her face, her sunglasses. I squint toward her sunglasses and clamp my mouth shut tight.

"Those photographers are probably here now. They're doing some candid at-home shots. I've got to go to them."

I nod. I hear her walking down the stairs, the swish of her sleeves.

I sit and I remember this, not minutes past. My mother sits downstairs, as if this were a hundred years ago. She sits before the snap and flash of a stranger's camera light. She turns and poses beautifully. He tells her, "Sigh"; she does. And "Smile"; she does. My mother's every gesture, every angle that the light finds on her cheek will be made permanent.

I put my hand around the glass she held, and recognize, just barely, how the light outside has changed. I sit in the seat she did, and look across at my now-empty chair.

I close my eyes and try to find her image there. For a moment it's light. Then dark.

Thus my mother hires me to research her biography: The Life of Lucia Holmes.

"You'll have to go through everything," my momma says. "You just do what you need to do. I never worry my little head with all those details the way those folks in promo do." Her voice is singsong. She smiles at me over the edge of the *Hollywood Reporter* she's leafing through. "But don't make me out too badly, darling. A gal's reputation can only stand so much and how rumors do fly!!" She laughs and shoots the paper from her lap with a clap of her hands. "How Hollywood just lu-*uvs* a scandal! Well, I heard of one myself just the other day. Now, wild horses couldn't drag it from me, but I'll just whisper a little tiny bit of it. Can you imagine. . ."

I turn off listening to her while I watch her arms billow like shadows in her pink chiffon sleeves, the shine of her just-manicured nails, the brilliance of her absolutely color-less glasses.

I set an office up in the library and go through notebooks and files and movie magazines. There's tons of it, piles and piles of it. Junk. Lies. My mother posing with famous stars, my mother in movie posters. My mother on the cover of *Life*, the cover of *National Enquirer*. Her nominations for awards, the year she got the Oscar, her generous contributions to humanity.

I see my mom's career, her image formed and nurtured by the studio ("They've been like family to me," she says in an article in *Star*), while I was away in Italy. They sold her image as an innocent unknown, this middle-aged woman who'd never seen a movie camera before, and all of a sudden she's got this huge part and pulls it off so well. And more important than that, she represents the success of any humble and hard-working Yankee darling. They all want to be like her.

The articles keep on and on about her humble roots, etc., but they never say exactly what her humble roots were. Did she not tell them?

There is no mention of her home, her family, or any place she ever lived before. No one, especially her, seems to notice what is lacking.

Because, of course, there's more than that.

Sometimes, when I'm careful, in between the promo shots of Lucia on location, I will find another shot, a half-developed print at the end of a page of proofs. Someone lurks behind her, in the folds of her Elizabethan skirt, her parasol.

"Shouldn't there be more, Lucia?" I ask one day.

"More what?" she bristles. "Haven't you got enough?"

She spins from me, a prima donna refusing an encore. I don't pursue her.

But of course, there is.

We're sitting on the balcony of her room. It's Sunday morning and we're in our robes. Her robe is huge and colorful and thick and mine's just like it. I've brought a tray of coffee up in the silver coffee server. The curves and round shapes of the pot are so pretty. I've even brought up sugar and cream, though neither of us takes it, just so that I can see the silver shapes together, the sun glistening in the little crystals of sugar, and watch the ghost lip of white that forms on the inside of the cream jar when I jostle it. There's fresh, home-made croissants and raspberry jam on the small china plates. I look at the crusty flakes of the croissants, then up at Mom, the yellow crunchy crumbs on the left side of her mouth. Her pointy sunglasses reflect the sun toward me. I can tell she's squinting by the wrinkles of her eyes I see outside her black frames.

I read the editorials and the front pages; she reads the entertainment section, Pesonalities on Parade, and the comics. Though sometimes she rearranges her tinfoil tanning mirror beneath her neck, stares up at the sun and whines to me, "Won't you be a dear and read the funnies to me?" most of our conversation is nothing much. Just grunts, reactions, "Listen to this . . . ," "You're kidding. . ."

I like the rustle of the paper when I fold it back. I like the way her glasses slip down her nose and the way she scrunches up her nose, then they slip again, and she unconsciously lifts her glasses up with the forefinger of her left hand.

"Now just listen to this," she says without looking up at me. "Someone writes in, 'Is it true that Diane Keaton and. . .'"

"Mmmmm, s'at so?" I mutter.

I only hear half of what she says, but I'm happy to hear that, happy that she's sitting there with me chattering about things I couldn't care less about. I like the way, when we're alone, she talks to me with her mouth full, the way she picks the crumbs of honey bun from the side of her mouth with her middle finger. I know these unconscious habits of hers. I've watched for years.

"My God, who's she sleeping with to get coverage like this? Did you realize this is the third week in a row they've had a question about Liz in the *Star* column?"

"Really?" I mumble, flipping the front section over to find the conclusion of an article on the oil embargo.

We drink coffee till it's lukewarm, the cream separate and yellow, the sound of the tourists' cars circling the mountain grown to a constant hum.

As I stand to go in and start her bath, she sighs behind me, "Hon, as long as you're up, would you start my bath?"

She hasn't looked up at me when she's asked this, just kept her eyes on the gossip page. And I know that even after I'm no longer on the patio, she'll mutter things like, "Can you believe it? Still chasing the Gerry and Lance story all over Beverly Hills. . ."

I start her bath and put in five drops of her favorite oil. I test the water with my wrist to make sure it's the exact temperature she likes. I pull out two fresh towels, and fluff them up. They're monogrammed LH in gorgeous script. When the bubbles are just about right and the room is steamy and smells of Autumn Musk, I head back to the balcony. Halfway across the bedroom floor, I see her outline through the lace curtains, and I freeze.

She's standing up, her back to me, and ironing. I hear the rustling of the newspaper and then her quiet laughter, which I no longer understand.

I tiptoe to the window and peer out through the blowing curtain. I recognize her body, the swing of the flesh on her upper arms. I see her familiar posture, slightly leaning on one leg. I see her graying hair fall long, her firm arm pressing the iron back and forth. My deck chair across the balcony from her has changed into a big orange corduroy armchair. Carefully as I can, I pull the curtain back to see more clearly. The chair is also turned away from me, but I see someone's angel hair above the back of the chair. I hear, over Edwin Newman's drone, their laughter. Then someone else's reading voice. She's reading an article out loud to her mother. My mother pushes back her hair.

I stand here, mute, on this side of the pane of glass.

"Mom?" I try to whisper, "Mom—"

I hear the paper rustle as I watch my younger body turn the pages. I hear my mother's iron move as if in stereo. I hear it twice: then—now, at once.

"Mom?" I try to ask again. "Mom?"

But I can't make a sound.

I open the door wide and stumble out to the balcony.

"I've always wanted a family. My dreams were simple. . ." My mother's profile up against the sky. It's misty gray, a gorgeous, soft-lit evening. I feel like I'm eavesdropping. I didn't mean to stumble on to her, but once I'm here, and hidden, I stay. She's all alone, thinking out loud. Her voice is tender, soft as tears.

"I only wanted a home I could call my own, that we'd never have to move from. I just wanted a simple family. . ."

She pauses, her lips closed. She lifts her head toward the mountains. I start to stand and tell her I'm here.

"All this is just the second best," she says eloquently, raising her beautiful neck, and sweeping her arms wide toward the luscious grounds of the mansion.

"Mom?" I almost speak aloud. Her face is radiant. I hear something—crickets?

Then she stands, stately, from her chair. Her voice proclaims, "I would have given all of this." Regally, she stretches her arms wide again, then lowers her voice to a sensitive hush, "just to have had someone to read the Sunday paper with—"

I stand up and wave to her. She doesn't look.

"All I ever wanted was one good, loyal love."

"Mom?"

She turns from where I stand, and looks out over the horizon, the gloriously red sun setting, the soft blue mountains that catch it like a skirt.

"Mom?" I start to say again. Then I blink. It's like the sun has risen again, and she's lit up from behind. She looks like a saint.

"All I ever wanted was the sweet love of a daughter."

Behind me I hear it clearly now, that faint insistent clicking hum.

"Mom?" I raise my voice.

She doesn't turn. I want to tell her that I'm here. "Mom!" I shout, "Mom!"

A voice behind me yells, "Cut!" The clicking stops.

"Terrific, Lucia. We'll print. Mark that 'LH at Home, Take 1.' Got it?"

My mother lights a cigarette.

I continue research on my mom's career. These photographs became the punctuation of my mother's life. They shot her "casual," "at home"; my mother lounging in her toga by the swimming pool, my mother having coffee in the parlor. My mother giving them the tour, my mother stepping into her limo to leave.

In some, my mother's hands are on her lap, around her glass of mineral water. Her glasses throw a shadow on her face.

But in other ones, some faded figures squat. They hover in her background, shadows, ghost images from somewhere else. These are the ones I look at most. In these her makeup's on too thick, the jewelry is heavy on her hands. In these, the props have been mislaid, or strangely rearranged. She's in a Viking dress for one of her awful historical plots, but the handsome lead across from her, though he wears an oafish helmet like Leif Erikson, has the sleeves of a leather jacket sticking out of his armor. When she's dressed like Cleopatra, one of the children stands out like a heretic, an angel wisp of white-blond hair.

"Who's that?" I ask, in the interest of my research on her career.

She snatches the pictures away.

My mother startles me in the middle of the night. She's standing outside my bedroom door calling my name out urgently in a stage whisper, "Robin? Robin?" I'm still not quite awake when I stumble out of bed and meet her in the hall. I'd thought the voice was in my dream. She's got a flashlight and shines it at me when she sees me. I'm naked and she offers me her dressing gown.

"Do you want to put this on?"

"Uh-uh." I'm still blinking. My arms are tightly clasped around my torso and I'm stooping over a little. I'm chilly and half asleep.

"You sure?"

"Uh-huh."

"I keep hearing something outside my room," she says, "in the yard. I didn't mean to wake you, but I want someone else to hear it." She sounds almost apologetic.

"That's OK."

I follow my mother down the long hall to her room. All the lights are on in her room and with my eyes just now adjusting, it looks even more light than it is.

We both stand there a moment as if we've forgotten why we're there.

"You can hear it best from here. I opened the window."

I follow her to the one open window and feel how cold it is out there.

"It does it every couple of minutes or so," she tells me, "I don't know what it is. What if it's someone hurt?" She sounds like a child. "Or an animal? Oh, that's it —" She catches her breath but not quickly enough for us to hear the cry distinctly.

"It'll do it again," she whispers.

My mother and I hunch by the drafty window and stare out into the dark. Now she's drawn her arms up too and is hugging her chest tightly like me. I can feel the warmth of my hands in my armpits and the cold against my exposed stomach and thighs. My skin begins to prickle up. I look out at the yard to hear the sound but I can't help watching, out of the corner of my eye, my mother. There could be anything inside her little robe tonight. She looks very small, like all that's beneath there is bones. I feel so different from her. Every part of my body is visible, naked. And then I'm thinking of how long it's been since my mother has seen the way I look, and I remember her always sitting across from me on the toilet talking to me when I took my bath until I was in third grade. And then I think how, though I don't remember any of this and I never will, she does remember me in my small baby body when I was her baby. I'm suddenly self-conscious realizing how much she has seen me and watched me, how she knows and remembers things about my body and growth, things I did and was, that I will never know and she could never pass on to me even if she tried to say them to me. Then I'm especially self-conscious as I think this because for an instant I think, if she knew all those things, then she must know everything, must even be able to read my mind, like right now. How could she not be able to, when she has watched my face and body and movement for so many years, since the time when I was inside of her, part of her body and then so close as to almost be part of it, and then when I grew away from it? I'm afraid she knows I'm thinking this and hug my arms closer to myself like I'm trying to keep this secret from her.

But then, quick as an optical illusion I see that my mother has no idea what I'm thinking, the only thing exposed is my body. She looks tiny and small under her little thin nightgown, like she's trying, in a pitiful way, to protect herself from something.

Then, both of us hear it.

It's not a sound like you could make, but it sounds like a sound you'd think about and want to make if you could because it sounds exactly like a way you feel sometimes but can't say.

"That's it!" she says. "What do you think?"

"It's not human," I answer, "it's got to be an animal but it doesn't sound like it's in pain. It sounds lost or something—"

"Or maybe it lost something?" Her tone is half question, half suggestion.

We don't say anything else, but stand there silent, waiting.

What I can hear is our breathing, both of us, and for a second I can't tell the two sounds apart, as if they were not separate. I also hear the whisper of leaves and another sound that is only the sound of night.

"Well, that's it," my mother says with relief. She turns to me and raises her arms in a so-what gesture. "I just had to have you hear it and tell me I wasn't crazy." She looks at me and when I don't say anything, her voice changes totally. "I've been hearing it for ages now, literally *ages*." She pauses. "Well, a few nights anyway." She laughs like she's at a cocktail party and I can imagine her at this party telling this story to a group of her admirers, her shoulders and fine neck bare, the fingers of her left hand clasped gently on the thin stem of a glass, the cigarette holder in her right hand gracefully punctuating the story from which my role has, without a trace, you could even say miraculously, disappeared.

"Don't worry Mom," I say carefully. She doesn't correct

me. "I heard it too." I want to smile to her and I think I do. I think she looks back at me with a certain look and I think we both know something.

When I'm back in my bed the sheets are cold and I realize how cold I am too. I pull the covers over my head and blow on my hands to warm them. I think of when I was a kid and I used to play forts under the blankets of my bed or stay up late and read by the clandestine light of the flashlight.

Then I'm thinking of my mother and how strange and large and square and white her room looked to me just now. I lift the blankets from my face and feel the chill of the air against me. I hadn't realized how long it had been since I'd been in her room, several weeks at least. And it's only a few paces from my room. Our lives take place so close to each other.

My mother is alone now in her room, in bed reading the *Hollywood Reporter* with her half glasses. I imagine her startled by the sound of this thing that is an animal looking for something. I remember her childlike voice when she offered me her dressing gown to keep the cold off me and how she looked when I walked behind her and the light from the flashlight cast shadows around her like a silhouette.

All of this happened only moments ago, but I think of it with the kind of sadness you feel for something long, long ago that you can't have again but you tell yourself you'd want to if you could. It's like looking through the wrong end of the binoculars and everything close to you looks hopelessly far away, out of reach, like something you can't touch.

Because I feel like we've missed something, my mother

and I. At least I know I have, and I think my mother must have too, because it was something both of us wanted, wasn't it? But maybe my mother didn't want to know exactly what I do; maybe my desire is too much. Maybe it was enough for her to know that someone else had heard it, but not need to know what it is.

But still, I feel something over me. Perhaps it is the sadness of not learning the name of the thing whose sound brought us together.

Days on end I spend in Momma's library reading through the history of her life in film. I read the folders that the promo office made, the exposés in *Star* and *Film*, the stills from MGM. But underneath these careful kits, I find my mother's kept her private stash as well. And it wasn't just the articles she kept. I think my mother tried to hold on to everything, the tickets from her openings, the apron that she wore in her debut, the call-back roster from her first audition, the check list for her screen test. I think she had a need to keep these artifacts, the evidence that, somehow, though the parts she played, the fantasies she projected, would be kept alive on celluloid, she had once been more than that. That she had had a past of flesh and blood, a life before she lived her life on screen.

These latter I find tucked away in tiny boxes, taped and sealed and labeled with abbreviations in my mother's hand. And pressed between these artifacts are scraps: pages with a child's scrawl torn form a looseleaf binder, photos ripped from albums, a dog collar, a ribbon for the first place at a spelling bee, two plaster casts of hands. And photographs, the punctuation of her history. In these my mother poses for the camera's flash while ghostly images rise behind her, haunting.

When she's alone, I catch her: "Who are they?" I stop her on the stairs, "Where were they going, Lucia?" I murmur in her window, late at night, "Do you remember me?" At the table when the china rattles louder than my voice, I ask her, "Tim?" When I pass her in the hall, I mumble, "Betty." I surprise her from behind, my rasping voice, "Well, hey commander." I shout at her closed window when her limo pulls away, "Where are we going, Mom?"

My mother startles me in the middle of the night. I hear her tapping on my door, calling my name out urgently in a stage whisper, "Robin, Robin."

"Mom?" I whisper from my bed. "Is that you, Mom?"

I crawl from my bed and tiptoe to my door. I lean up against the cool wood and hear her breathing inches from me on the other side. I look down at the crack beneath the door and see the shadow her feet make, blocking the light from the skylight in the hall.

"Mom?" I ask again, through the solid, separating door, "is that you?"

"Hurry Robin," her voice as secret as an intimate. "Hurry."

I put my wet palm on my doorknob and pull the door open. In the gray light of the skylight, my mother's profile looks so pale. She gestures me to follow her.

"Do you want a robe?" She nods at my chilly, shaking body.

I shake my head "no" and follow her through her house. In secret, holding our breath, we scurry through the halls, hoping we won't wake anyone.

Our hearts race as we fumble at the lock on the library door. Before we enter, we glance behind us, furtive. We slip inside.

Inside the room is waiting for us, furniture.

She sits me on the couch right next to her. I feel her shoulders sag when she sighs next to me. Then, so quietly that I can barely hear, she holds me close, puts her lips to my ear and tells me, "Yes, dear daughter Robin, I remember."

She pulls them out, their covers soft and pressed and printed with dates and names.

"I always used to be afraid," her voice no louder than her heart. "I used to be afraid, with all the moving, that we'd lose them. I remember I used to wake up in the middle of the night, just snap up awake and panic — where were they? Where were we? I couldn't remember where the basement was, or the attic, which town we were in. I'd wake up and not remember where we lived."

She swallows. "Because I wanted them. I used to think if I kept them, I'd have them. Even when they started taking up room, and it was hard to pack and move them all, I wanted them. I didn't want to lose them, to forget."

Her fingers open up the covers slowly. "These are the postcards you sent me from Italy. This is the article about you when you got the scholarship, and here's the one about the design award."

My mother has kept everything.

"This is the little essay I wrote about you when you went, the picture I took when you got on the plane."

I've never seen this one before. It's blurred, like wet. My mother snapped me from the back, a hundred yards away and through the airport window as I left. I stand on a step to board the plane, my back to her. I'm leaving and I don't know how she's watching me.

These photographs became the punctuation of our family's life. In these photographs we sit, the three of us, in living rooms in countless boring towns, the military bases where my father had his orders. Mom and Tim and I on the old orange couch, the corner just below the white border scratched through by Prince Lexington's nervous paws. In this one, Tim's and my faces are smeared black with liquorice around our lips. We're sitting almost in our mother's lap, our heads poised over the page she's reading to us from. Tim and I in junior high and high school, his acne-splotched face and mussed-up hair, his pursed lips looking away from the camera. In the early ones, my hand is on his shoulder in protection, the later ones we stand apart, staking out corners of the frame. My mother and I sift through pages and whisper like spies, back and forth:

"This is the house in Jacksonville."

"This is the house in Norman."

"This is the time we drove out West."

"This is the summer it rained."

"This is the suit that Princy tore."

"This is the Ford we drove."

We whisper back and forth till I go back no further. Then I watch my mom caress another cover.

Her voice is quiet as I've ever heard. She opens the cover to an empty page. There're gray tiny marks in squares where tape had held the photos once. She points to a blank space on the page.

"Do you remember this?"

I shake my head. I can see nothing there.

"This," she points, "is your father." Her hands cast a shadow over the page. Her voice describes a picture I can almost see on the dim gray. "His skin was smooth as a baby's, his hair so full and blond. . ." I almost see my father's face rise from the empty page as if he's looking straight ahead to me. I almost see his jacket, his crisp white shirt, his straight dark tie, his lips full and puffed at once. There is a tiny rise between his chin and jaw. His angel eyes.

"Your father and I were married in Oklahoma City at the end of the Second World War." My mother's wrinkled hands spin circles above the blank page. "Here," she says, pointing to nothing, "in the Rogers Courthouse." She runs her finger horizontally and recites, as if she's reading captions. "Nice?" she asks. I nod silently. She turns the page — it's blank. "Then we moved. . ." Page after page, the book is blank. My mom describes the pictures I can't see — her wedding and my birth, my infancy, town after town in which she lived alone or just with me when I was too young to remember: the first years when her husband left, the birth of Tim.

That's when her voice gets small. Her fingertips are careful on the page they almost touch. "He was so little and tiny. He had the softest skin of any baby ever born. His skin was so white you could almost see through it. His hair, so soft it felt like water when I touched it. At first I didn't want to comb it. I didn't want anything to touch his precious head but me.

"I used to worry about him so. He was so little and sick all the time. His knobby little knees and hands. And he was so quiet. He'd just drift off to his room without any of us even noticing he was gone. Even then, he was like a ghost."

She points again to the empty pages and asks, "He looks like one, doesn't he?"

"Yes," I lie to her. I cannot tell my mother that I see no photographs. "Yes, I do remember that," I lie again.

"And I remember you," my mother says.

She looks at me but I keep my tired eyes on the closed book cover.

"You were going to be just like him. I could tell that from early on." I know she isn't talking about my brother. "You always wanted to be somewhere else, romantic. Never where you were, but where you'd been, or someplace you imagined."

"That's not true," I want to say to her. But I don't tell her anything.

Because You're Always Wanting to Go Back

To then?
No, back before.
To way back then?
Before.
Before these things had happened?
Yes. But way before, before we knew they would:

Before the time when things began to fall, before the fall. Before the time when we knew things could fall. Before the rise, before the flight, before the letting go. Before the sadness or the loss. Before the words, before the longing for the words. Before the mouth, before the lips, before the yearning thighs.

Before the empty images, the gray. Before the flash, the harsh, before the waiting dark. Before the sharp departing and before the riddled flight. Before the birth, before the break before the photograph. Before the thought of break, before our brutal, innocent conception, and before the night. Before the want, before the cry, before the awful knowing. Prior to the touch, before its loss. Before the quick undoing of the flesh. Before the need for solace and for words. Before the separating and before the time of grief. Before the death, before the birth, before the separation into two. Before the time of parting and before the time of wanting to go back. Before the break, before the cut, before the need to make a word for loss.

Because there's something she can't say:

"The loneliest I ever was, was when I was with you.

"It was that beautiful day, that gorgeous beautiful day it rained in Kansas City. It poured and everyone had to stay home. You couldn't see beyond your front door. The air was all sheets of moving gray, like slate. So we all sat inside. We built a fire and all sat together in the living room. I sat on the couch watching you two kids play on the carpet. Your father was home, and you were all laughing and having fun as if he was home every day. You just laughed and rolled this ball back and forth. I was sewing up some socks. You were dressed up so cute in those little red velvet jumpsuits and playing with that ball and laughing with your father as if he was there every day. You didn't know the difference.

"I looked at you two and you were happy. You didn't know if I was there or not. It didn't matter to you. And I realized as I watched, that I'd see things about you you would never know yourselves. I'd love you in ways that you could never know. And that would make no difference. You could never love me back like that. I realized there was no one.

"There is a special way to see someone, a way you see the things they do. They will not even notice them: you will. You will remember.

"I saw the way your tummies changed, how long Tim kept his baby fat, how long you chewed your nails. No one else would ever know the sudden, drastic, overnight transmuting of your legs, how I tucked you in as a toddler and you woke different, walking, suddenly skinny and angular. No one else will remember the shape of your bottoms when I changed you, both of you, for years. I remember the way your tiny baby shoulders fit into your back, the round soft cup of the pit of your arms, the tiny turn of your throat. I remember the way your baby skin changed, the touch from cream to rough. I remember the fresh soft way your breath was when you slept, how small your fingers were, how small your fingernails. I watched the dimples on the backs of your hands turn to knuckles, hard and lined. I remember the places your skin got sore when I bought you a pair of shoes. I remember the little scars on your back from the summer of chicken pox. I made you little mittens so you couldn't scratch yourself in your sleep. I watched you sleep. I sat in a chair next to your beds and waited for you to turn and kick the covers. I pulled the blankets over you again. I held your heads when you were sick. I woke up when you wanted a glass of water. I held your sweet warm head when you drank. You slept through it all and were dreaming again by the time I left your room. But I lay in my bed and thought of you, the fierce and utter tenderness I felt for you.

"I wanted you to need me and I wanted you to stop.

"I wanted to be free of you — the awful tug of need and love, the brutal love of need, the vital, awful dragging of my heart.

"I never have been loved like that. I won't believe in love like that again.

"For we outgrow this perfect love.

"And, despite the wanting to go back, we can't. And soon we stop remembering what we want. We just recall the wanting.

"When something truly goes away, you cannot get it back. And nothing else is like it, Robin dear. There is a lack, an empty shape no other shape can fill.

"You never could come back to me. Dear Robin, when that first thing changes, everything then must. You learn to measure out each getting rid, each keeping. Loss isn't choice, dear Robin, it's just loss. There's no again, no going back. You learn to live with what you have. You learn how to forget."

Did my mother look at me? Or hold me? Did she carry me? My sleep-drugged body heavy as a child? I don't know. I don't remember when she left. But suddenly I found myself alone. Surrounded by her artifacts, the things she tried to keep. I closed my eyes.

I go through all the footage I can find of her, TV appearances, clips of early screen tests. I watch her movies from the start of her career, bit parts of maids, one of the ingénue's girlfriends, a pretty chorus girl. Then, her more substantial roles, and then her break to stardom. I watch her change from the flashily dressed girl to confident career woman to matronly teacher; I watch her get old. In the earliest film, an old black-and-white, she wears a tight-fitting, low-necked dress. The material shines. It's suggestively thin, her high-heeled shoes tight and pointed. Her hair is bleached blond and it swings when she walks, or rather bobs along, pretty girls never just walked in those days. She is all energy and smiles.

In her first talking part, she has only one line: "But you can't say that," which she grossly overacts. Her eyes are too big, and her gesture — she spreads both her arms out to her sides — looks cardboard. I wonder how this movie could have made it, but it did. I look at the old clip in the flickering light and read about what a box office success it was. I can't believe anyone ever took any of this seriously. I don't kid myself for a minute that things were really the way they showed them. The plot is contrived and nothing is at stake. You never believe anyone is really in any danger and you never really care about anyone's emotional life because there is no emotional truth. My mother's one line fits in with the generally awful acting of the whole movie.

But people did believe it; they wanted to. Part of me gets sad at the thought that it's not just my mother's innocence I'm watching, but the innocence of a whole group of people, a country and a time, that I am distant from. My mother and her audience believed things that I never have. I try to find them in between the stupid things they say to one another in the movies.

My mother in her silly black dress cut so close to her hips

and thighs, and her brilliant black lipstick that I know is red in real life on the set, her firm young legs, her bouncy platinum hair, the girl's lilt in her voice, "But you can't say that" fit perfectly. Even if whoever my mother is addressing when she tells them they can't say that, does say that, it's not so bad. The things they worried about in those days were "How could anyone, and I mean anyone, be wearing a jacket like that?" or, "Is Rog really going out with that Stevens girl?" Not being able to communicate meant not knowing how to follow your boyfriend on the dance floor.

In the enclosed light of the screening room, I watch my mother's first tiny fling with stardom. I try to think what she must have been thinking when they picked her out of all the unknowns on the set and asked her to do the line. I imagine her at home telling her mother that she'd gotten the most wonderful part and who knew where it could lead. I picture my mother in her room that night standing in front of the mirror saying the line to herself over and over in every possible way, milking it for all the subtle nuance she could squeeze out of it, every innuendo and suggestion. "But you can't *say* that!" My mother fantasizes that she will do a perfectly spontaneous ad lib so snappy and clever that right then and there the writer and director and producer will sign her up for something grand, a big part, co-authoring the next movie. She points to herself in the mirror and smiles, "But *you* can't say that!" She puts her hands on her hips and shakes her head back and forth, "You *can't* say that!" She realizes that this line means everything, and the more she thinks about it, the more it means. She watches herself in the mirror and is at once shy that her mother downstairs will hear her practicing, but also excited and proud, wanting to show her mother her performance of this soon-to-be-unforgettable line from the history of American cinema, or at least my mother's history.

But she didn't live with her mother when she broke into film. No, her mother wasn't there.

I'm watching my mother say her very forgettable line in a screening room in the elegant home she's bought with her movie money, many famous movies later. The image flickering on the screen is yellow and fuzzy. It skips erratically, then stops. For a second, everything is dark and I can hear only the whirr of the projector. I snap on a light to fix the machine. When I do, the entire room feels different, like the temperature has changed. And I feel funny too, like I've walked into the wrong home by mistake. I want to turn off the light again and leave, pretend I haven't invaded. But that's silly, I tell myself, I'm alone in this room with a movie projector.

I fix the projector and run the rest of the reel through, knowing there is nothing more of my mother in this film. I watch the film on the reel grow and think that somewhere in there, the frames of my mother are whirring round and round. My mother's going around like a Ferris wheel.

I feel cheated by the permanence of this film. My mother exists whether anyone is looking at her or not. She's dormant, but you can call her up at any time. Then I think of all the films she's in and I feel dizzy and confused thinking how easy it is for anyone to conjure up pictures of her, but more than just pictures, part of her, to look at any time.

I put in the next film and wait for it to roll. I know this movie, as I do all her films, by heart.

I don't have to watch the film all through, but I do. I let

myself get completely caught up in it and try to see it as if I'd never seen it before. I act surprised and delighted when something happens. When my mother makes her first appearance, I pretend I don't recognize her, as if she were just another one of the girls. I wonder what she looks like to anyone. Would anyone pick her out from all the other girls: Is she pretty? Does she have the mark of a star? Would I want to meet her? I trick myself by concentrating my energies on one of the other characters in the film. In studied nonchalance, I pretend my mother strikes me no more or less than any others in the movie.

But I can't. I'm drawn to her. What really gets me is the little gestures, every move she makes. I watch the way her skirt swishes and the lines in her cheeks when she laughs. I listen to her voice and think how it sounds alike and different from when she talks to me. I want to walk into the movie and tell them I know something they don't know. But I don't want them to know what I know about her: I want that for myself.

When she smiles at the little girl in the film going off to summer camp for the first time, it's the smile that belongs to me, which she gave to me when I flew up in Brownies. When she talks to her neighbor about the dog going into the garden, it's Shirley, our neighbor in the apartment. When she gets in the blue Nova it's our yellow, beat-up Ford. When she goes to the supermarket, it's our Safeway on Grand. But I'm not in the picture and her husband is not my father. She does some things my mother wouldn't do. She doesn't shop like that, or iron. But the way she takes the pot roast out of the oven and puts it on the table, it is my mother.

I remember the way she used to dress and act and look.

She is younger and her hair isn't gray. True, the color in the movie is exaggerated and her hair is browner than it ever was, but it isn't gray. Her body is different. It's the way she carries herself. She slams the car door the way I haven't seen her do in years. Her voice sounds like it used to. There's hardly any of the falseness I hear in it now.

I watch the movies, including the one that got her the academy award. The part is grueling and her performance is astute, marvelous, perhaps even brilliant. In this movie, more than any of the others, I try to separate myself from her as my mother, and appreciate the role for what it is. I'm moved. For an instant, I actually forget she's my mother and I want to congratulate this artist on her marvelous creation. I want to know everything about her and learn things from her. I want to tell her I know how important her work is. I want to tell her how she's spoken to me. But I can't say that.

Because I feel a surge, remembering who she is. I've been fooling myself. In fact, the only way I ever look at her is as my mother. I want her to be that to me.

When this movie ends, I'm staring at the screen. All the credits go on in front of me and I watch them blankly, not registering. The only image in my mind is of my mother, beautiful and tragic and graceful in her final seconds in the film, speaking something so moving I can't even hear. But I don't need to. Her expression tells me everything I could know.

The film runs out, but I don't stop the projector. I'm lost in the image of this actress, my mother.

It's dawn. I've spent all night in here, this room in Mother's house. I almost have forgotten where I am.

Behind me, the door opens.

I don't turn around, but I know it's her. I know she's standing in the open door of the library, and behind her the morning light is shining brilliantly, lighting up her hair. She walks to me where I'm leaning over the projector, exhausted.

She puts her hands on my shoulders and says to me, "You are my daughter, Robin dear. You are—" And then—

No. She says, "I know what you want most to say to me, dear Robin, and I know the most beautiful things in life must go unsaid." I turn to her, reach out my hand, and then—

No. That isn't what happens at all. What happens is the door opens and I turn around to see her. Only after I flash her a confident, yet humble, grin and say, "Hey, Mom," do I notice she's been crying. The notes I've made for her TV biography are scattered all around me and there are bags under my eyes because I've stayed up so late and worked so hard for her. "What's the matter, Mom?" I start to stand. She runs to me, her purse sliding down her arm, throws her arms around me and sobs, "Oh my faithful daughter, now I know you are true. Your conscientious work has proved to me your honor and unflattering loyalty as compared to all the others who come and go. Truly you are. . ." etc. And then—

No. What happens is she says, "Don't look at me! I can't bear for you to watch me as I tell you how awful I have been. My whole life has been a test of you. Oh, please forgive me, my darling daughter. I wanted so much and I couldn't believe it was possible. I didn't believe it till now. But now—" I smile my serious, understanding smile, more like a saint than a human being, and I say, "There, there, my mother dear, I understand." She sobs and we leave the library together. I hold her, and I carry her, her body heavy as a child. Outside the sun is brilliant and we are blinded by light. And then—

No, no, no. That isn't it at all. She doesn't come to me. What happens is, I run. I run. My legs pump as fast as they can. My heart is racing, about to burst. I'm going to find her. I'm going to catch her. I'm going to tell her. I know she's working in her studio. I know she doesn't want to be disturbed—she's never disturbed in her studio—but I know, I *know* she's waiting for me to come to her. I'm going to. Yes, I am. I'm going to come to her and say—

I run to her studio. She's there. She looks beautiful. Everything's in place and I know I ought not to interrupt everything with my wild exclamation, but I'm going to. My hair has been blown back and I look windswept. I'm breathing heavily from my dash to her. "Mom!" I shout, halting at the door, my arms spread out between the door frames. My breast is heaving and I'm gulping air. She looks at me and in that moment, everything freezes.

Part of me tells myself what a fool I am, and why do I always have to go off telling people things they're embarrassed to hear? And why do I get so confessional? And why do I get all flustered and caught then tell myself to cast politeness to the wind and just say it, while at the same time tell myself to hold it in and not flail myself so much?

I run to my mother's studio. I am filled with urgency. I must tell her now. I stand in her door frame, my breast heaving and I'm gulping air. "Mom!" I shout. My mother looks at me, stares deep into my eyes. And I know I see her too, beneath her sunglasses. She reaches her hands to her face. And everything gets frozen.

No — In that moment, everything freezes for me, but she still goes on, only in slow motion. I see her turn slowly around in her chair, her sleeves billowing under her. The sun catches on a brass box on her desk. When she sees me, she slowly breaks into a rapturous smile. And —

No. She looks startled and then enraptured and —

No. She looks calm and placid and — no — she doesn't even look up. No. She spins around looking all flushed from her concentration. And when I look at her she knows — She knows — I say — I almost tell her, "Mom —"

No. No. Not even that is what I want to say.

Because she isn't really in her studio. At least, I don't find her there. I run up to her room. Not there. I stand in the doorway to her bedroom and listen. Silence. Just my exhausted, panting breath. I run down the hall to my room. She was here, just yesterday, in my chair and telling me, "Now, Robin hon, I just wouldn't. . ." I spin around and rush back to the bathroom off her bedroom. I know, I *know* as soon as I round the corner I'll see her soaking in the suds, her face pouting because she can't read her *Hollywood Reporter* through her steamy sunglasses.

But she's not there.

I dash out to the balcony, our two lounge chairs, and the blown-over remnants of the Sunday *Times*, caught in the railing. *Where is she?*

Across the valley, I see it's starting to rain. The sky is gray and I am gulping air. I'm desperate to find her, but I'm gulping air. I flop down in my lounge chair to catch my breath. I close my eyes.

When I open my eyes, the clouds have moved in closer. I suck in a big deep draft of air and rise to leave the balcony. I step into the sliding glass door and start to head into her room, when I turn around again. I walk briskly back out to the porch and see, yes, it's gone. Her lounge chair has disappeared. I lean over the balcony rail and look down into the garden. The chair hasn't fallen off. I'm sure that when I sat down to catch my breath, it was there. I turn back to her room.

To see the bed is stripped, her dresser and her mantelpiece bare. I rush to the hall to see who's carried off her bedclothes and the knickknacks from her room. But the hall is empty. Even the paintings have been removed. I spin back around and look in Mother's room. Now her smaller furniture is gone, the curtains taken down. I run down to the second floor. All the guest rooms are empty, not just of guests, my mother's fans, but furniture. The house is emptying. I think the house is moving.

I stand still and try to listen. Do I hear the legion of her friends, her chorus boys singing Broadway musicals as they pack the vans? Nothing. Just the clean and bright house echoing, emptier and emptier around me.

I tear down the carpeted stairs to the first-floor landing. The door is open and the sun streams in, bounces off the perfect parquet floors and almost blinds me, the harsh light bursting through the clouds. She'll have a hell of a day to travel, I think, and strain to hear if I can hear her trail of limos, Bekins vans.

I close my eyes and see her sitting in the car, her sunglasses slipping down her nose, holding her *Hollywood Reporter* as if she's reading it.

But she's looking somewhere out in front of her, or back, the eyes reflected in her sunglasses.

I don't know where she's going, but I hear her telling me, "There's just one way to beat them leaving you."

I stumble back to my room to pack whatever I have left. I'm going to follow her. In my empty room, the furniture is gone. The walls are bare. My feet slap and echo. And, curtainless, the windows look like lozenges of light. They pour soft round white color on the floor.

In the center of my room, on the still-wet, just-mopped floor, a flight bag Momma's packed for me. I bend to pick it up. It's heavy and it clinks. I open it. Inside, more bottles than I've ever seen, glinting down the bottomless well of the bag.

I close the bag up tight, zip up my flight jacket, and stumble from my room.

I'm going to follow her and bring her back. I swear I will.

I follow her around the world.

Because every time I blink she's moved again. To Turkey or to Thailand, then to Rome, Bombay or Monterey. I don't know where she's going, when she goes, or how she gets there, but I follow her.

I land in foreign countries I don't know. They speak different languages, and not a word's familiar.

I look for you.

I chase people down the boardwalks. "Have you seen her?" I beg, my eyes wild with greed. "She's my mother," I say, knowing they don't understand or believe me. But I pour out boxes of your photographs, the promo kits, and ads. I recite the deathless lines from your most famous performances.

They shake their heads, "Non capisco, non capisco." But sometimes they gesture wildly and point: I know I've only missed you by an instant.

I run. I think I've seen your sleeve, the hem of your dress disappearing around a corner, your shadow falling from a roof, the glint of your sunglasses. I hear the echo of your laughter from a small café. I know I've only missed you by a moment, or a day.

But I know you're out there somewhere, Mom. I know that you exist. You have to: How else could I get away with signing your famous name to all these credit-card charges unless you were picking up the tab? In fact, I think you book these trips for me, so I'll arrive in Biarritz or Monte Carlo, Arlington, a day or hours after you've departed. It's gotta be you, dear Mom. I know it is. And someday I'll catch up with you. I will, dear Mom. I'll find you. Yes. I'll be there, breathless, panting, waiting in your makeup room, your dressing room, your room, waiting to bring you back home. I'm on to you, dear Mom, I've got your number.

I'm walking on a beach, sweating, clinging to my movie posters, my movie-star bubble-gum trading cards. The sand feels gritty in my shoes. I sweat. Sweat runs down my eyes. It's hot. But it's a gorgeous day and I feel good about it. This one's going to be the one. I know. I don't know where I am.

I look up at an open-air café raised above the beach on stilts overlooking the waves. I see her. I see her lift the thin stem of the champagne glass of mineral water to her lips. Her sunglasses.

She's sitting with someone under a big wide colored umbrella. I see his brilliant, fresh white jacket, gold braids on the shoulder, his brilliant white hat and black brim shining in the sunlight. He's raising a glass to his lips under the umbrella. I can smell it now—bourbon. He's wearing dark sunglasses too.

I watch her order round after round for him. This should take time, but suddenly my vision has the properties of a camera and I see the next two hours unfold in time lapse: all in seconds. She's not saying anything—just guiding him. He smiles, beautiful and cool at once.

Though I'm a hundred yards from them, below them on the dirty beach, my vision's like a zoom lens. I see his cracked lips sip his sweaty bourbon, while she taps her finger on the tabletop, her other hand poised on the thin stem of her glass. When she lifts her dewy glass she leaves a cool crisp ring of steam. The tabletop is glass and clear. They sit together looking out. I turn around and look behind to see what they're looking at—nothing. Ocean. Green-blue waves. I turn back. I think I almost see them speak. They almost speak.

Though I can't see their angel eyes behind their shiny sunglasses, I recognize the wrinkles on their cheeks. I start to try to shout to them. My mouth is open almost saying— But the instant I do, the instant I try to call her by her true name, the instant I call her "Mo—" I'm whisked away. Like I'm on the other end of a zoom lens shooting out. I'm yanked away. I'm shot back through the brittle wind. I don't know where I'm going.

I try to grab the formless air. I can't. I struggle, fast and terrified. My eyes bulge open, dry. I fall. I scream. But I don't land. I never land. I just keep falling, caught and sharp. I try to scream out, "Mom!" I'm falling. "Mom!"

I gasp — the air. I choke — the water in my lungs.

Do they hear something at the beach? Do either of them move?

So this time, goddammit, I'm taking it into my own hands. I'm going to trick you. I'm going to anticipate your moves and beat you there. I'm going to fly.

I sneak to the airport. But when I walk up to the ticket counter, I see you. You never go to airports anymore, but there you are. I pretend I'm only there to see you off. But I'm damned if I'm going to do so in proper Hollywood style, crying goodbye and flailing my tear-stained, monogrammed hanky at you. Instead, I nonchalantly squeeze the arm of your white fur coat, and wink so suave and debonair into your dark sunglasses, "See ya, baby doll."

I turn briskly and strut out the door in my Italian shoes.

But I don't leave the airport. I circle back. I duck into a bathroom and quick-change into the nerdy leather jacket and thick, black-framed glasses, white socks and scruffy penny loafers. My heart leaps when I walk through the electronic surveillance gate. I try to smile innocently when they wave me through. My hands sweat when I ram them into my pockets.

In the waiting lounge, I sit across from you and watch you light a cigarette. You do it exactly the way you did in the remake of *To Have and Have Not*. You suck in your cheeks when you inhale and look around to see if anyone recognizes you. You clear your throat a couple of times and keep looking right and left. You don't see me. You shuffle in your bag and flip through the copy of *Star* with your picture on the cover. I strain to hear the man behind the counter tell us where this flight is going, but he doesn't.

I sit next to you on the plane. I feel the feeling of tight and full, the taking off, and then, the letting go.

I watch you from the corner of my eye flipping through *Variety* to an advertisement of your newest release. You leave this open on your lap, close your eyes, and pretend to sleep. I can almost hear you listening to the whispering around you. You don't recognize me.

When I'm sure you're actually asleep, and I hear you snoring the way I used to in the tiny apartment in Arlington, I lean over and shake you awake.

"Gosh, ma'am," I say in my sweetest, star-struck voice, "are you the star, Lucia Holmes?"

"Yes," you sigh to me, like a queen.

"Gosh, Miss Holmes, I'm sorry to wake you up, but can I have your autograph?"

"But of course, de-ah, I'm only too happy to oblige."

"Gee. I've got my high school yearbook up in the closet. You wanna come there with me and sign it, Miss Holmes?"

"Why certainly, darling." I know your thinking this will give you a chance to flounce around the cabin and have every-body notice you.

"My name's Robin Daley, Miss Holmes," I chatter as I follow you through the aisle of the plane. You laugh your trilly laugh as if you're listening to me, but you're nodding to your fans as you walk by, a regal presence deigning to mingle with the mob.

And I'm tricking you. I lead you past the closet. You don't notice because you're smiling graciously and waving to your public with your parade wave. I lead you to the front of the

plane, crack open the cockpit door and shove you in. I fling my crooked arm around your neck. You choke. You almost fall. I flip the pistol from my pocket and cram it into your neck. I sneer to the back of the solo pilot's head. "OK, joker, this is a hijack. Take me where I want or Little Miss Star gets it right in her pretty Hollywood face."

You're writhing beneath my arm. The pilot nods silently. "Where are we going? Over," he mumbles through his beautiful flight scarf.

When I hear his muffled voice, I jolt. I loosen my grip around your throat.

"Where are we going?" he asks again, his words a slur.

I knock you on your knees and squat behind him. My breath is quick. "You know where I want to go, goddammit."

"I'll fly, you navigate," he says. "Tell me how to get there. Over."

He turns to look at me, but I twist my face away from him, his scarf. I jerk my other arm around his neck and start to choke him. I knock his breath of booze right out of him.

"Goddammit, I mean it. Take me back. Over."

He gags when I choke him and his hands drop from the controls. The whole plane jerks.

We all fall forward. I grip my shaking arms tighter around your necks. I hear both of you gurgle.

You rasp, "Let him go, you idiot fool. This whole thing's going down."

And it is. I feel the quick descent, and hear the burst of bright flame on the angel wings outside. I start to sweat.

"Where are we going?" he tries again. I feel the tendons and the muscles in his neck move underneath my arm.

I want to tell him where I want to go, but our descent's so rapid that my voice is knocked from me.

"Let go of him, you idiot fool," you whisper, desperate. "We're all going down."

I tighten my grip on your necks and feel both of you squirm. Your dark sunglasses tip awry. Your jacket's cracked with heat. I twist my head to see the cockpit door behind us has been ripped away. I can't see to the starless sky, just this hot solid wall of flame. I imagine the way we look from the ground, a cone of falling flame. I close my eyes and grip both your necks tight, then tighter, tighter in my loving arms.

3

THE HAUNTED HOUSE

Our windows look like lozenges of light. They're tall and wide and high. Curtainless, they run the length of every side and pour soft white round color in the yard.

Carrie and I strip the hardwood floors. Like everything, we make them bright, the way we want. All our lives we've waited for this place.

Some evenings we sit on the porch and look out at the land. Arm in arm we walk to town, admiring our neighbors' homes. We point out details, what to use, what to avoid — that angle setting off the sash, a color that reflects, an archway where there should have been a door, the pretty twist of wrought-iron gates, a porch.

At dinner we read out a list of things we'd like to do. At night, exhausted from our work, we sleep deep, close and soundly.

We work reconstructing this old home. Our bodies change. Our shoulders, backs and stomachs firm and tighten. I cook in the evenings; Carrie cleans up after our day's work. Sometimes I listen to the radio, but other times I leave the kitchen door wide open, windows too, and I eavesdrop on Carrie. I hear her sneakers in the dining room, first muffled then squeaky, as she sweeps away the fine mute covering of sawdust. I hear the final quiet lick of brushes spreading one last coat of yellow light on old dark walls. I like the sound, her filing off the bottom of a door, the rough soft buff of sandpaper on paint. I can barely hear the swift scrape of her pencil on the board she'll cut, and then the whirr of blades. I think of her back made wet, the film of moisture mixed with dust, her happy and unconscious hum while she restores our home.

I can tell from the sound of her brush and tools, just when she stops to think. I know exactly how her head will tilt, a little up to her left side. Her mouth will open slightly as she looks hard at the rough sketch on her clipboard. When I hear, or imagine that I hear, the swish of her sleeves, I know she's stepped forward to the bench again. She'll shift the weight from one leg to the next, and put her finger to her lips in concentration. Then she'll lunge.

Sometimes I have to snap myself back to my task, or I'll stand there half an hour, staring, without seeing, at a pile of ripe tomatoes, pasta rolled out flat and waiting to be cut, a bunch of fresh oregano, just listening to Carrie. I feel kind toward these things, protective of their crisp and uncooked colors. I want to treat them tenderly. I chop them, throw them into pans and cover them.

After dinner, we walk through the house and, as if we're seeing it for the first time, point out to one another all that's new: the pretty varnished banister, the bright knob on the door. We say we like the polished brass, the way the light will catch against the shine. Carrie nods abruptly, pulls my arm to see the next accomplishment.

But mostly what I think about is her, the way I know her back curved when she leaned to stroke and stroke again the wood, the pressure from her palms.

"I like it here," she tells me, "this old house." She turns from me and squints down at the floor.

"We're making it over," I say. "This time we're making it wonderful."

I don't know if she hears. I want to tell her something else, but forget before I've even got the words.

And then I'm glad I don't because she's squatted on the floor and runs her finger on a dusty molding. She mutters something I don't hear. I don't ask her to tell me.

She asks me, "Robin, what do you remember?"

I look around, the flat brown prairie, wide wild open sky, the brittle air. I shake my head.

Our house is on land out of town. We walk the short miles into town and drive the faithful beat-up Ford just when we must. The plain is flat and dry at night. The red-orange sunset is a flame beneath the lip of earth. There's grass that's brown and wavy, waving toward the homes on either side of us, both several hundred yards away, white-painted, wooden homes like ours. There's a one-lane road about fifty yards from the front porch. The cars that pass belong to neighbors whom we only know as "There's the Ramblers!" "It's Mr. Dodge!" "Well hey, it's Mrs. Pontiac!" Our skinny pole mailbox is old and rusty and gray and round and huge. When we first drove up to look at the place, Carrie said, "The Pony Express used to deliver to the Sooners at that box."

"It belongs in a museum," I said.

"Or here," she answered with a grin.

"Roger," I told her, "over and out," and laughed.

Because it had never changed, we didn't change it either. So it stayed.

At night the whole wide sky is stars and you can see forever. It's pitch-black, brilliant white at once. Some nights we just sit on the porch and hear the world breathe.

Our neighbors on their porches wave to us. In shops we pick up cord and wire, buy brushes, paint and groceries. Behind me, when I'm counting out my change, I hear them whisper, "She's got his angel eyes . . . I'd recognize them knees most anywhere . . . her neck. . ." I turn to ask them whose and they don't answer.

We giggle when we leave, and mimic their tobacco-chewing jaws, how they suck in their cheeks, or raise their eyes.

Their families know each other from way back. How someone's grandpa cheated someone else's when they made the Sooner run, the great-uncle who tricked the cards the night before the raid. They whisper one another's secret histories; the unclaimed babies born out back, the half-wit's mother's bargain with the shoe salesman from Tulsa. Brothers who took brothers' wives, the fathers who ran off. They say,

"Well, that's just Jackson orneriness." "Them Spivys always were the wanderin' kind." Or spot a Nelson chin a mile away.

Carrie and I laugh between ourselves and try to imitate their accents on the way back home. I've got the knack, but somehow Carrie doesn't.

For months we sleep and wake to work. While I make coffee, Carrie writes a list. We hold our steaming cups and give ourselves assignments. Sometimes we work together in one room and chat or listen silently to the other's gliding movements with a brush, a file, a saw. Or we'll listen to the radio, the same old jokes, commercials, twangy songs. And sing along with all the sappy choruses.

When we work apart, we listen for the other one's approaching feet, or shout aloud through the whole house. We chatter about nothing just to hear the sound of one another's voices keeping brushstrokes company.

We make up excuses to find the other in the room she's working on:

"What did you say you wanted the trim to look like?"

"Hold this so I can see if that's how I want it."

Our faces get powdered, flour-white, or gray smudged where we've cleaned a musty closet. Sometimes our whole bodies drip with color, paint spots, lines of stain. In the shower, we rub colors on and off each other, watch the pretty streams of green and blue, the thread of black that swirls down the drain, the faint cool rose that leaves a tint.

Our windows, curtainless, let light go in and out. We like the light reflected on the bare bright-shined wood floors.

What we've discovered: layers and layers of wallpaper with patterns of tiny flowers and curliques, hunting scenes and lavender brocade, pale coats of green and beige. We peel off layers of skins of walls that watched a family grow. Then leave, forget, remember, and return. We peel back this home's skin gingerly, as if we are disturbing, interrupting, dusting off the cover of a grave. We pull up floors, flat rugs and carpets, strata of linoleum. We knock out tiny windows, let in light, build skylights into gray cold stuffy rooms.

We mark our time by our work here. Instead of saying "last month," it's "when we worked on the study"; "this morning," "when we hung the pictures up"; a walk to town, "when we bought that new cord."

The colors of our house:

The kitchen walls are sun-bright gold, the dining room, bright blue. My study is a pale brown, Carrie's a sweet soft peach. The halls are creamy white with trim. The bathroom navy, blue and sky. Our room is rose and cream and rose.

The porch and the outside have stayed the same — new coats of bright sharp white that catch the sun. At different times of day the colors change. The house looks pale when evening falls, and radiates a flush when morning comes.

I like the way that Carrie looks when she's in each of them. She smiles in the kitchen, pours herself a glass of juice. In my study, she's quiet, knocks first, tiptoes in and leaves without a sound. In the bath she lies on her tummy, grinning while the water makes an aqua pattern on her chin. In her own room, her skin looks round. She hums content and confident at work. She moves quick, undistracted, through white halls.

In our room, her body feels like a petal.

We're smoothing drywall. I watch Carrie's perfect detailed hands, the flexing in her upper arms and shoulders.

I watch her wrists get tight. She smooths the drywall perfect in her corner.

"How can you get it so smooth?" I ask, leaning toward her work. "Mine never looks like that."

She squints toward the corner, looks back at me, then places her flat palm against the wall. When she takes her hand away she's left a print. "OK," she says, "now you," and takes my hand and puts it in the plaster next to hers. Side by side our handprints look like they belong to the same person.

"There," she says, "we'll know it's not all smooth and perfect under there. It'll have our own little signature."

Our marks look like the plaster casts of hands you make in kindergarten.

"And that's not all," she tells me suddenly.

She pulls me around so my back is almost at the wall. "Hold it right there." I roll my eyes up as I watch her place her blade flat on my head. Her palm is on my head. Her voice, "Now stay still, honey." She makes a mark of my height on the wall.

"Now you do me." She pulls me away from the wall, spins herself to where I stood, and straightens her shoulders high. She giggles at me.

"But neither of us is going to get any taller." My voice is puzzled.

She shrugs. "Just mark it and we'll always know it's there."

I mark the line her head hits on the wall.

She stands back and with her index finger writes the date and "R" and "C" next to our marks.

"It'll always be there, no matter what gets put over it—this will be underneath there too."

I nod.

"Will you remember that?" she asks.

"Roger." I nod again to her.

"It's our *home* now," her voice is firm, "nobody else's. *Ours.*"

But I can't answer her.

We've been here months. Carrie goes to town to shop. It's early, when the morning light lights particles of last night's dust kicked up by me when I walk in the room.

The light is strong and pink and white. It almost looks like flesh. I know the empty room is bare, but I think I see shadows. I turn behind me, back again and rub my fingers on the window hoping something in the glass is casting shapes.

I turn and face the room again and feel the hot sun beating on my neck, the clear heat soaking in my skin. When I open my eyes it seems brighter. The only sound is me. I try to imagine Carrie's walk, her window shopping at the hardware store, her friendly chatter with our local grocer.

I set up the ladder and start to open a can of paint. Then, instead of pulling a knife from the pile of tools, I slip a pencil from my pocket and walk toward the wall opposite the window. I squat down on the floor, and on the glaring brilliant empty wall, I start to trace a shape, the pencil's scratch, the only thing I hear, then I don't hear. I kneel up and pull the pencil slowly. I stand and move the marking to my left, an arch, up, half a moon, then down. I'm back again, against the ground. I stand up straight, take one step back and stare.

The light changes to afternoon, but I don't notice.

I'm startled when I hear the screen door slam.

"Hi, hon!" It's her. I hear her putting things in cabinets. I don't move.

Then she's behind me. "So how'd it go today—" She stops and looks around the room. Still unopened cans of paint, the brushes clean, the footprints in the sawdust left from yesterday.

"What have you *done* all day?"

She looks at the faint gray pencil mark I've drawn across the wall.

"There's a fireplace back there," I hear myself whisper.

She walks to the wall, squints, runs her palm on the pencil line.

"How do you know?"

I shrug.

"Do you remember anything?"

I shake my head.

That evening we work through dinner, then the night. We put our dust masks on, our caps and gloves. We break and drill and cut the old tough wall. It's there—an old stone fireplace beneath the layers of plaster, wood—a skeleton.

Carrie says, "You knew. How did you know?"

But I can't answer her.

There's more. A staircase that leads up inside a wall to nowhere. Sealed passages, locked doors, windows that look out themselves to — nothing. Frames that once were windows. All of them now covered up by walls. All of them we find beneath my tracings.

We break down walls and stumble over relics; a broken cup, a baby shoe, a beat-up leather jacket. Stacks of movie magazines, a pair of dark sunglasses. Photo albums, toy propellers, canisters of film.

"Throw it out," I tell her.

"We haven't even looked at any of it —"

"Toss it," I snap. But I've been too harsh, because Carrie's giving me a puzzled look. I try to pick it up and laugh, "Over and out. Over —" But she won't laugh.

We sweep and wipe out dust and cobwebs, stale air. Every place we can we put up glass, surround ourselves with light.

At night I concentrate. I try to make the only sound I hear be Carrie's breath.

This evening on the porch, we drink champagne.

"Are you cure you want to do this?" Carrie asks.

"This once will be OK. Hell, it's our housewarming."

I watch her face when I pop the bottle open. I watch the pure white smoke and drops hopping off the surface. I inhale deep and long. We toast. The glasses clink. She starts to put the champagne to her lips. I stop and clink my glass to hers again. And then —

"What's that!"

"What's what?" she asks.

"You didn't hear it?"

"No."

"It sounded like a crack."

"It's just the house settling."

"That's it," I echo, hoping.

We toast again and drink.

"To home."

"To home."

Today's the day that we've been building to.

After the second bottle, we sway, giggling, from room to room and put on all the lights. I know our home shoots beams across the yard, sharp lines of light that thicken into bands, then widen into soft and edgeless shapes, warm rolls of white that soak into the night. Our house looks like a bundle of the sun.

Carrie and I, arm in arm, dance through our home. A lindy in my study, a twist in our bright kitchen. We do the tango in the bathroom, back and forth, while the water's filling up the tub. We laugh and make up verses, rock ourselves to sleep, a close-armed waltz.

I almost sleep the whole night, then I don't. I think it's the champagne that wakes me up. I slip from bed and tiptoe to the bathroom where I splash water on my face and drink a long cold drink. I look around at everything in order: the bathtub tiles we replaced, the mirror by the sink, the dark blue trim, the shiny white ceramic knobs. It's perfect and it's ours. I'm convinced there's nothing we've forgotten.

Smiling to myself, half-smug, I wander through our finished house and crack the door to the back porch. I gulp in deep drafts of air. Outside the yard is bathed in silver light and Carrie's sawhorse looks like it's a toy. I walk through piles of neatly stacked-up wood, the tools we've left. The night smells green and gray and fresh and everything is silent. I listen to the lick of dewy grass against my feet. At the far end of our property I look at our good solid home outlined by moon. It's so quiet I think I almost hear dear Carrie breathe.

I look up at the open sky and see a falling star. I hear the whirr of falling flight. I see a fading arc of white, and then, the sky is blank.

When I go back, I sneak in bed beside her. I tuck the covers under Carrie's arm and watch the outline of her neck and chin. The covers rise and fall so slightly I can barely see them move. Limp cool ribbons of moon cut our bodies into dark and light. The moon at the end of the bed makes it look like we wear socks made out of light. I laugh to myself quietly and tell myself I'll tell her in the morning. Then, gently, careful as I can, I pull her heavy sleep-drugged body to me. I wait till I too find again my deep and hard-earned rest.

At breakfast Carrie says, "You're tired. You didn't sleep?"

"I did. But something woke me up."

"What?"

"I don't know."

"The house is settling."

I nod.

"Well, we can both hang out and rest all day," she tells me with a grin. "There's nothing else we need to do."

I don't say anything.

"Hey," she says, "come on, isn't this the part of the movie when we're supposed to say, 'this is the life'?"

I try to nod, but feel my shoulders shrug.

"How about, 'there's no place like home'?" she valiantly attempts another line.

For her, I smile, and say, as if I'm catching on, "No place."

I spend the morning in my study trying to catch up on letters to my old friends. "Dear Davey, We've finished the house," I write, "and now . . ." But then I don't know what to say. I start to write Max anecdotes: *Life in the Sticks*, our redneck neighbors' accents and the way they watch, the time that funny old man just stared and stared at Carrie and finally came out with "Long way from home, aintche?" Max would be amused if I confessed, in mock repentance, that we've actually learned to like country-western music. Janet would want to know how pleased we are that the house fits in so well with our portfolios.

But I feel like I've forgotten to whom I'm writing, like it's been years since I've seen any of them. I can't recall their faces or why I felt so close to them back then. I am forcing friendships I've forgotten.

I try to read a book but can't concentrate. I wander to the kitchen, stare in the refrigerator. I look out the window. Carrie sits on the back porch swing and reads her book. She blows her breath across her coffee cup. Her calves get tight when she pushes her foot to move the swing. One hand is wrapped around the cup, the other holds the book still in her lap. I stand in the open door.

"What are you up to?" she asks when she hears me behind her.

"Oh, hanging around."

She puts her book down in her lap. I look out at the garden and I feel her look at me.

"You're restless. You've always got to have some little project, some distraction. And right now you're just coming down off the house. I mean, we did eat, sleep and breath it forever. Here," she pats the place beside her on the swing. "Come on, angel, just sit with me for a while. You can bring your book out later."

"I can't concentrate —"

"It's nice and quiet."

"I know."

"Besides, who needs to concentrate today? Take it easy for once."

"It's cooler inside," I mutter, as I put my hand against her neck and feel a film of sweat. "See?"

"Mmmm," she purrs, rubbing her neck against my hand. I massage her neck till she closes her eyes, then wander back to my study.

In my study, I pace back and forth to my big orange chair. I flip through three books before I settle down. I read the same page twice, then close it.

Each thing in this room is still and quiet; the yellow bronze crescent of the doorknob, the vertical colored bars of books on shelves. I miss the comforting whirr of drills, the whack of hammers, our exaggerated, happy shouts.

Outside I hear a tiny squeak in something short of rhythm, Carrie's movements in the hanging chair.

I sit as quiet as I can and run my eyes over the surface

of my room. Then I concentrate, a random choice, the second row of the bookshelf, and only the ones to the left of the divide. I look and look and when I think I've pulled it in, and nothing could erase this out of me, I close my eyes. Then I try to remember.

The whole sight recurs exact, immediate: each book, each spine, each faintly inked-in title, the way the last one leans against the next, the different heights like skylines of a city that I almost recognize. The vision of my memory moves up the olive backs of tall fat books, the broken spines of paperbacks. I trace the horizontal of the deep brown shelf, the change of texture where it meets the vertical. I feel like I can feel the things I see.

But then, eyes closed, I'm so inside that I forget I'm anywhere. I see these shapes and colors, shades, these textures and I don't know what they are. What is the name of this flat thing, this white that crinkles in my hand? What is the meaning of the black marks on the white, these gray shapes in this tiny square, this round shape that's a color I've forgotten? I forget the words to call them. Then I'm terrified. I've nothing I can hold on to. I can't touch or call them back. Then from somewhere back behind my head, I sense that there's a secret to uncode these things, a click of light that could tell me their meaning. I forget my eyes are closed, that I knew names before I knew this silence.

Then, from outside, I hear a sound, a squeak. And then I am reminded. A tiny squeak, repeating back in rhythm. It's the sound of metal springs. It's swinging in a hanging chair.

So, I remember words: "chair," "sound." Then I remember someone's name; it's "Carrie."

Carrie works on her portfolio each morning. She shows me her sketches and sends her drawings out again. The afternoons when it's too hot, she sits on the porch and reads. She listens to the radio and hums along.

"I've always wanted a place like this," she says. "I knew someday I'd have it."

"You do," I say to her, "you do."

But lying next to her that night, I watch the light that squeezes in through limbs of trees, the patterns forming on our bedroom walls. I listen for the rustling whispers in the leaves, the half-words in the creaks of this old house. I run my palms down Carrie's back and gradually slide my hands away from her. I move as if I were half whispering and leave her in the bed alone. Outside the room the whole house feels electric. I wander to the kitchen, open the refrigerator and recite to myself as if it were a necessary project, "More eggs, running low on OJ—" I shut the door when I realize I'm just staring. I watch the flag wave to the national anthem and listen to the tiny scratchy noise of the volume all the way turned down.

The next morning, Carrie finds me in the chair in front of the TV. I'm sleeping and she jolts me.

"When did you get up?"

"I didn't."

"What?"

"I didn't go to sleep."

"What's wrong, angel?"

"I don't know. I heard something I think."

"The house."

I shrug.

"It's settling," she tells me. "It just takes a while to settle."

"It's too quiet here," I say softly. Then I shout, "It's too quiet. Do you hear me? Too screaming quiet!"

"I hear," she clutches my arm.

"I'm not talking to you," I snap.

"Then who?"

I jump up from my chair and turn on the TV. "Now this is what we ought to be hearing." I point to the weather forecast, the price of hogs splashed on the fuzzy screen.

"You take a nap this afternoon," she tells me tenderly. "You're really wiped out."

She goes to the kitchen and brings us juice and vitamins.

"Thanks," I mutter. Then I look at the TV and say aloud, "Too quiet here. You got it? You listening? Too quiet. Over and screaming out. You hear?"

She doesn't ask me who.

I take a nap that afternoon, drifting in and out of sleep. The scrape of Carrie's pens, the squeaking of the swinging chair, both comfort me and keep me restless, half-awake, aware. I turn on the clock radio beside the bed and float half-conscious, dreaming to the muted buzz of country songs repeating their old theme: faithless women, booze, trucks, trains.

I want to sleep, I know I should. But the room's too light and hot. I feel like my body's being coated. My hands make solid fists around the sheets.

I finally sleep and wake almost refreshed when I feel Carrie nestle into bed.

"You slept all day. You needed it." She snuggles up to me.

"I didn't sleep. I mean, I did, but —" I put my arms around her. "What did you do?"

"It was a good day. I finished that Rec Center plan so I can get it out when they want it. And I actually like what I did with it."

"That's great."

We fit around each other and the space between is small. I stroke Carrie's head till she's asleep and then I stretch my hand in the air above me. Rectangles of moon-white gray spread across my forearm. I open up and close my fist and listen to the snapping in my fingers. Carrie turns but doesn't wake. It's quiet everywhere, but I hear something. I look over the whole gray shadowed room as if I'd see something I had missed. I close my eyes and try to sleep.

In the bathroom, the light is bright as shock. I turn the water on and listen to the gurgle from the pipes, the clear clean wet of sloshing in the sink. I'm relieved I see the thing that makes the sound. I splash cold water on my face. I lean toward the mirrors and I look, as if I'll see the dim retreating figures of some foreign inner country fading back into my frightened eyes. But all I see is my familiar, startled face. I pull my skin down on my cheeks to make the bags beneath my eyes smooth out. I shut the tap off slowly, listen for the final drip, the last sight of a drop of brilliant wet.

I walk through the house, each room, and listen to my fingers on the light switch. I don't see anything that's strange, but when I turn away and shut the light, I think I almost hear a sigh, a syllable, the dark.

Before I return to bed, I stand in the hall outside our bedroom door and look back down the dark unquiet hall. I can't see the end of it or where the angle turns away from me. I can't see what holds its breath. And mine.

I'm careful of my footsteps when I crawl back into bed. Not that I'll wake Carrie up, but that I'll disturb something else.

The next night I stir up again and wander through the house. In the kitchen I snap on the radio and fumble through the static for a station. Late-night preachers, talk shows for the lonelyhearts, I can't find any music. I turn the volume up, hoping I'll get something from far away. Then suddenly I hear a cymbal crash, perfectly and clearly. I turn the dial slowly thinking I've discovered a classical station. Then it clangs again, but behind me. I spin around. A tap, like metal on metal. I stand in brittle silence, then it clangs again, above. I turn my eyes above the stove, where Carrie's hung our pans and pots on a rack suspended from the ceiling. They move. First one against another, almost randomly. But the more I watch, the more they move in unison, in rhythm, side by side, a chorus line like something from a musical. Left to right, then back again, they ripple. The kitchen door's not open; there's no breeze. I scrape a chair across the floor and hoist myself up near the rack. There is no draft. The pots move of their own accord, or like something else were pushing them. My face is inches from the colander. The taps are slow and tentative, a child trying out a triangle.

"What are you doing?"

I spin and almost topple off the chair.

Carrie's in the doorway, half-awake. She rubs her eyes and yawns. "What the hell are you doing?"

I stumble from the chair and stand beside her. I point to the rack, now still. "Those pots and pans and things started to move."

"What do you mean?" Her voice is tense.

I whisper, awed, "I was standing there trying to find a station, and I heard them. I looked up and they were moving."

"So?"

"But there's no breeze. They just started moving by themselves."

I stare up at the glittery shiny shapes.

"Hey," she passes her flat hand in front of me, "it's no big deal. Don't make it such a big thing."

"But there's something —"

She pulls me from the kitchen and leads us back to our room.

When we're beneath the covers, Carrie sleeps. I close my eyes. I hear leaves fall against the glass. I hear the restless arid night get cool. And just before I fall, I hear another sound I almost recognize.

For something wants in this house. Outside the black dark window, something pulls.

And this time both of us wake up.

"What is it?" Carrie whispers.

"I don't know."

In the morning we both look for signs. There is nothing either of us sees.

A few nights later, Carrie pulls away from me. "It's here again." Then she puts on a light.

In the dim round yellow of her bedside lamp, we see shadows thrown across the room. The dresser drawers look black and gray, like giant slate-gray mountains. Carrie's face is peach and white. The outline of her profile hums with light. I pull the covers on my skin and hunker deeper underneath the quilt.

And then, beneath the floor, we hear what woke us; a tentative, insistent sound, of something that is trying to get through.

Carrie pulls her legs out from the sheets. She leaves the bed and paces slowly on the floor, her finger to her lips in concentration. When she turns to me, she says, "It's here." She kneels on the shiny wooden floor. "Right here," she lays her bare palm on the spot above the urgent noise that rises. I watch Carrie's body hunch. The pale yellow on her skin looks gold.

We listen to the faint insistent noise.

"It's here," she says more certainly, "there's something underneath the house that's scratching to get in."

I watch Carrie listening, her serious, firm brow.

"I think it's something caught within the crawl space."

"It's never happened before," I whisper, feeling every caught breath on my tongue.

"It could be rats."

"Raccoons?"

"It could be cats."

"It could be anything."

"Just settling."

We listen long enough to be convinced the sound will get no louder, that whatever creature craves the warmth and light of our room will not break up into here through our thin, fragile floorboards.

Carrie tiptoes back to bed beside me. We don't touch. She leans up on her elbow to turn out the light. I think I hear, beneath the sound of whispered scratching underneath our home, a tiny *phhht*, the incandescent wire going out.

Long after Carrie sleeps, I lie there listening.

The next day I go into town and order carpet to cover every floor. I come home with a heavy bolt of cloth and spend the whole day in my study sewing.

Carrie brings me dinner where I'm bent over the machine. "It's late, angel."

"Sorry," I mumble. I hear her sit behind me, but I don't stop running the material through the machine long enough to look at her.

The sewing machine rattles.

"Why did you get this?" Her voice is raised above the clatter.

"Curtains," I almost shout.

"I thought we didn't want—hey, can you turn that thing off for a second while I talk to you?"

I hit the switch but keep my eyes on the cloth I'm pushing through.

"I thought we didn't want curtains." Her voice is careful. "We didn't want curtains before."

"We didn't need them before," I snap.

"What?"

I turn around to look at her and try to gesture matter-of-factly. "It's just so noisy here. I mean, so quiet. This'll soften it up some."

I start the bobbin up again. I feel her walk up behind my back. She takes the end of the maroon muslin and rubs it in her hands. "It's so heavy. It doesn't go with anything we've got in the house." She runs her fingertips on the white-pine table I'm working at, then squats down on the floor so she's looking up at me. She raises her palm to my cheek and strokes my skin. I keep the machine running.

"What are you trying to keep out?"

"They're just curtains," I insist. Then I'm flip. "You know, curtains, hang in front of the windows? As in drapes, etc.?"

When she bunches the cloth in her hands, I see the tendons tighten in her wrist. It weighs more than it should.

I work nonstop the whole night through and hope the clang of this machine will drown the sounds of other things that I don't want to hear.

When I finish them, it's morning. I wake Carrie. We go from room to room in order, raising them. We put them up and then, just to see if they work, we close all of them. The rooms look thick and covered and the house feels like it's closed, almost protected. I fold my arms across my chest and pace before the tight drawn drapes. My feet are muffled. Cotton soaks the sounds.

"I think they'll do," I nod to Carrie.

She looks back at me. "I hope so."

"Well." I throw my shoulders back, as if we're satisfied. "No reason to keep them closed during the day."

Then we pull the curtains back and every room pours in with morning light.

That night when we've both closed our books and Carrie says, "It's time for me. I'm turning in," I touch her, "Carrie, listen." We both stop. "It's going to be different now. It really will."

She runs her fingers through my hair and doesn't say a word.

After she's left the room, I walk the whole house, room to room, and pull the drapes closed tight.

* * *

But in the morning with the curtains drawn, our rooms look halfway gray. The sun-bright yellow kitchen turns a sickly mustard shade, the hall's a dirty smoke, our room a faded bronze, my room, dull beige.

"It's not the way I wanted it to look," I say.

"It's dull because you're blocking out the light."

"I want it like it was," I say, not listening. I try to sound deliberate, logical. "We got good paint. We followed the directions."

"Look," she says, "it's the damned curtains—"

I turn away from her.

"OK, OK," her voice is hard, "do what you want with your part of the house, but leave some of it alone. Just some of it?"

I cover all the furniture in my study with white sheets. My shrouded things look like I'm planning a long trip away, or I'm just coming back. The limp uncolored sheets make hulking shapes. I almost wouldn't recognize my desk, my big orange armchair, the flat and billowed skirt on all my books: all this here to protect my things while I repaint my fading room again.

I try new mixes out, new brands. I try to get the color I remember. But each coat's just a pale variation.

When I sit down to rest, the armchair creaks beneath the cloth. I find myself quick-frozen, hand caught sharp midair, the brush poised still and silent. My heart beats. The whole room seems to move with my inhaling. I run my fingers on the unfamiliar cloth, trying to recall the smooth warm leather I'm almost forgetting. I tell myself I know what's underneath these sheets: the wood grain of my desk, the spines of books, my photographs, the round legs of my chair. I watch the white unmoving shapes and then I watch the wall, the thick uneven coats of paint.

I don't know if my watching makes it happen, but the second time I look, I see a filament, a tiny hairline break. It's careful, delicate and poised. My study walls are cracking.

"Carrie, something's happening." I bring her to my room.

"Look," my fingers point up to what looks like a cobweb. We squint at the corner of my dusky curtained room.

"It's there," I say, "a crack."

She nods.

"Settling?" I ask her, tentative, hoping she'll agree.

"It's more than that," she says, "you know it's more than that."

"And you do too."

From then on I know Carrie's watching too.

I cover up the crack with paint, and cover it again.

My study reeks of paint, and though I've closed the door, soon the smell is seeping through the house.

Carrie's breath is quick. She runs into my study without knocking. "There's another one," she blurts.

"What?"

She pulls me to our room: the rose walls etched with fine dark lines.

We start, together, repainting our room.

"It shouldn't be like this," she cries.

I listen to our brushstrokes, desperate, turn the radio up.

When we sleep, we breathe the sticky air of new wet paint. My breath is tight. I hear clicking from behind the walls, beneath the floor.

I wake to creaks: the rub of stone and sand, concrete, the tired stretch of steel, and the ache of wood.

I sneak from bed and hope that Carrie sleeps on undisturbed. I wander with a notebook and a flashlight, hoping I'll predict where it will happen next. I don't want her to know how bad it is.

And it isn't just my room, or ours. And it isn't just the paint.

Soon we're sweeping plaster bits, the tiles that fall out.

"But this is our house," Carrie moans, "it can't do this to us."

"The house was here before we came."

"But we remade it. Everything you see in it is ours. The walls are covered with our paint, these windows are new, the curtains to protect—" Desperate, she recites a list as if its length will outweigh what we see.

A chunk of plaster slips away behind her. Her voice is unbelieving, "But it's *falling down*."

She presses my flat palm against the wall. Beneath my skin, I feel a chill, an echoed rumbling, then still.

"There's something else that we don't know."

She pulls my hands in hers and holds them tight.

"You never expect things," Carrie says, "you forget that things can happen, but they do."

I look far deep down in her eyes until I can't see more, just her sad unbelieving fear, beneath my own reflection.

I pull her with me down the hall and point.

"That's new," she chokes. "It just happened. How did you know?"

I shrug.

"You know before it happens, but you don't."

I don't know what to say.

"You say you want to keep it back, but I think part of you wants to watch it. Do you?"

"I don't want this—" My words jerk out of me. "Remember what I've done with the curtains, the carpet. I want us to be safe—"

"This house is haunted," Carrie says, "and it's seeping into you, my love, to us.

"Look," her words are quick, "we don't have to stay here. We can get away from here. We can. Come with me."

I draw her to me in my arms and hold her tight as if I held her close. Neither of us sees the other's face. I whisper to her shoulder words from somewhere I don't know. But they seem so right and they sound so sweet that I tell her and I tell myself over again, again, so each time it seems less a lie, "It'll be all right, just give it time, just give it time and it'll be all right."

But each night I slip from our bed and stumble through our cluttered house. I pick my way through sawhorses and broken glass, piles of fallen plaster. I look for signs of where a new crack's due: a shift of furniture, the slip of frames, the slide and dip of books upon our shelves.

When I sneak back to bed, I lie there quietly, trying to decipher sounds. A creak — I think, the cabinet in the dining room? A ping — the screen door bouncing up. A snap — the corner of a shelf that's popped.

I close my eyes and try to breathe as if my heart weren't racing.

I lie away from Carrie fearing she will sense my restlessness. I do not want to wake her.

But one night after there's a crack, I hear her gasp and know that she's awake. I don't turn, but watch her from the corner of my eye. She's lying flat and staring at the creaking ceiling of our room. I see her open, terror-stricken eyes, the shiny half-moon curve that's caught the light. She weeps and holds her breath. I lie in the dark an inch from her, pretending I don't see, that I'm asleep. When involuntarily, I sigh, her eyes snap closed and she pretends as well.

We lie in the dark pretending we don't know the other one's awake. Pretending we can't hear or see. Pretending we forget.

But one night when I crawl back from my rounds and try to sleep, I can't. Then I hear Carrie slip from bed. I know, like me, she's on her secret, separate mission in the house. Like me, she's writing her own list of things she thinks will fail. I press my eyes closed tight and hear her restless pacing in the hall, her snapping on and off of lights, her solitary weeping while she tallies up the breaks. I try not to listen, either to our home's demise, or to Carrie's careful record of it. I wanted to believe she was immune.

We try not to acknowledge what we each believe in secret to be true: our precious home is falling down around us.

But one night on my secret watch, I turn the corner in the hall and see a beam of light. Tentative, a pale yellow wash that searches. Then it jolts. That beam and my beam brighten as they merge. Then I see Carrie's form outlined behind.

"What are you doing here?"

"What are you doing here?"

We avoid each other's eyes and shift on our feet back and forth. Neither admits we've each been keeping our own separate vigils. But, bound again after so long, we follow one another through the house like secret comrades, bumping into each other, almost touching. We're always looking back, behind, as if we are afraid we're being followed. Beneath our pale struggling beams, we try to decipher our pathetic scrawls.

"Last night I saw this corner crack—"

"I heard the first break underneath this rug—"

"I saw the window jolt—"

"The front door warp—"

"The hallway lurch—"

"The bathtub shift—"

"The couch—"

In the crooked light of our two beams we try to read each other's ashen faces. Carrie's lips and hands look gray. Then, as if our speech were dim, we lean toward each other's skin. Her lips are by my ear. I feel her cool breath near my neck. We whisper like we're trying to keep this secret to ourselves.

"When did it begin—"

"I don't know—"

"I forget—"

"I don't remember—"

"I forget—"

"When—"

Then we repeat syllables that we don't understand: the sounds of paper peeling back, a window's snap before it cracks, the shift of plaster under paint, the break.

"We'll meet back here tomorrow night."

"Till then—"

"Till then—"

We slap each other on the back like co-conspirators, co-pilots, stars.

She sneaks back to our bedroom like a spy, her head held low. I watch her evasive path, her dash from hiding place to hiding place. She ducks behind a fallen beam, below a shaky scaffold.

I go back by a different path, but no less carefully. I listen for the snap of wood behind me.

When I crawl into bed I hear her fake the even breath of sleep. In the few hours until daylight, we lie, wordless, next to one another in our darkened home. As if we'd never been awake, or had forgotten it. As if we hadn't met each other, desperate, lost and trying to break the pattern of our breaking home.

We don't want to admit that in this bed.

For each act of forgetting, there is something that comes back; for every act of memory, a loss.

We wake up to the sound of our house breaking. We stumble over saws and sawhorses, a pile of tools. We prop 2 x 4s against each other, angles pressing into empty space. We hope the walls will hold themselves apart. Each room of ours is cut by beams and braces. Sawdust covers everything. Our goggles, face masks, rulers litter all the floors. Our boots raise clouds of thick unsettled dust, make footprints on the ground.

As soon as either of us hears a crack, we rush to plaster it. We wake and sleep to smells of plaster, caulk and dust, and dress accordingly. We protect ourselves with masks and hope the air that we take in is pure. Some nights I wake to Carrie's rasping next to me, her muffled gasping underneath her dust mask. Her profile in the dark is powder-white. Her lashes look like snow.

We're afraid of what our house does when we sleep.

We try to make sure one of us is awake all night to keep our watch. We sleep separately, in shifts. When I wake after she's asleep, the living room's been moved. The ceiling opens to the sky and all the stars look in. The wall beside the bath, a gaping hole. I'm hasty, toss up drywall, plywood panels, covering.

We leave each other notes: "The west wall in your study might go next," "I heard a rumble underneath this corner."

"When will it settle down?" she scribbles. "What else can happen now?"

I don't know," I scrawl. "I don't remember. Over."

After a time, a note from her: "You're slipping. There's more cracks every time I wake. I don't think you want to work at this."

I lug heavy panels, wobble, crashing into walls. I scrape the sticky paint and bump rough corners.

I can't remember what this house looked like before we had to prop it with supports. Somewhere between these hanging planks, behind these hollow walls, was where we thought we'd live.

Our hallways now are labyrinths. We lurch through home, our shoulders stooped. Each room's divided into small dark caves. The colors of the walls are all in shadow, windows, curtains covered up with grime. We stretch our clawing hands through crooked spaces in between support beams trying to brush over cracks. We can't even reach them all.

When Carrie leaves the bed, she wanders, crumpled blueprints in her shaking hand. She mutters, "Can't we just get back to this . . . If we can just get back. . ."

I lie in bed and hear her tap her pencil to her clipboard, her valiant, failing will to keep this home.

I doze in snatches, something unlike rest, and hear the sad sounds—Carrie's whirring blade, insistent file.

But some projects require both of us. We work together, trying to balance what we reconstruct. Then fall, exhausted, back to bed, and set the clock so one of us will wake. But sometimes we both sleep the whole shift through and wake together, terrified, our bodies leaden, sheets made heavy by a coat of fallen dust.

These nights, we struggle in our haunted bed. Carrie's haggard face is over mine, her frosty brows and lashes. I almost remember what her smooth lips were like beneath the caking dust. I try to brush her skin.

I stop her. "Carrie, tell me that you love me."

She pulls her fingers from my matted hair. I hear her watch me in the waiting dark.

"It's not enough." Her lips move in her silhouette.

"Tell me anyway."

She pauses. "Yes. I do."

"Say, 'I love you,' Carrie."

"I do."

"Tell me the words."

Hesitant, a whisper, "I love you," each word a separate syllable.

"Now tell me you'll remember me."

She strokes her plaster-coated fingertips across my paint-splotched skin. "I will, dear Robin. Yes, I will."

"I love you too," I rush, as if the words will act like magic, two matched missing halves of rings, the two lost links that make the whole chain, one whole. We want to hold together. And we hold our breath and wait. And wait. And try to keep ourselves from wanting more.

Then, as if to stop ourselves from seeing what's not there, we hold each other in the dark, just for a time, and act like we believe. Our separate hands and mouths, our thighs, try hard to find each other and they almost do.

But I feel like I'm sitting right behind my head, and watching, on a movie screen, my tired arm raised in a tired fist, my fading smile trying to encourage. But I keep turning back and looking, something like a shadow over me.

I know each move of hers from memory, but not because it makes sense to me now. She hesitates and gropes. I do the same. Our sadly uninspired breath can't move us anymore.

For when her body urges me "Forget, forget," I can't. There's something else remembering in me.

And when we pull apart, we are relieved. On our sides, we lie apart. Behind my back, I think I hear her move, and I move too. We each acknowledge, silent, to ourselves, that we can't even comfort us again. Our bodies drift, reluctant, but predictable, apart. This sad attempt is finally our undoing, this very act complicit in our separateness.

* * *

Between our backs, our bedclothes gently loosen, slowly pull away. I reach my hand behind my back to feel unknitting threads wave a good-bye. Unattached, they move like underwater plants loose from the ground. I hear the quiet rustle of unraveling, a sound like water ebbing back from shore. But then it's fast — too fast — a rush, a tidal wave that bursts and heaves up from the rumbling earth below. The house trembles and breaks, the bed. The ground beneath us rips apart. I clutch the tattered sheet on me and turn to look for Carrie. I feel so heavy when I try to lift myself, like pressure weighing down. But Carrie's miles away from me. Receding from me fast, I barely glimpse her shaking body and her pale, terror-shot face mouth words to me that I can't hear. The ground she's on moves back from me, like it's sucked in a vacuum. The earth is two sharp cracked-off parts divided by a ragged, widening cave. My insides press and I'm thrown on my back. In space, I spin on my cracked half of bed. Below me is the shattered earth, around, above me, disembodied waves and falling air. My half-sheet billows, torn, in front of me, covers up my mouth. I gag — a flight scarf soaring, falling in the dark, loose and almost free. But I'm so hot, I can't breathe anymore. My eyes bulge out. I open up my mouth, almost saying something to her, then the air is sucked from me. I think that Carrie's lost as well, away from me, caught breathless in the dry cracked airless sky.

We wake up wet.

My face is moist, and Carrie's too. Her thighs and breasts and hands. Our skin slaps and we leave prints on each other's flesh. We move against each other slick and try to touch behind the slippery film. We can't. Carrie's wet face tastes like salt. She gropes for me, but cannot hold. My palms slide off her.

"Wake up, wake up," she's pulling me. "The house," she cries, "it's everywhere."

We wake up wet.

Her hands are on my shoulders and she shakes. I smell it everywhere. The blankets, damp, wring wet around our arms and legs. Carrie tries to pull herself away.

"Oh God," I moan and try to uncling from our bed. The ceiling sags, the bottom of a bag where wet condenses. The plaster's ripped like canvas. Water streams down walls. The floorboards heave beneath the weight. Our house is being flooded.

Thick liquid forms itself to tears and drips down from the roof. Carrie and I run from room to room, throw pots and pans beneath the largest leaks. Carrie gathers up her precious things, her family photo album, notes and drawings. She runs, dropping her sweet possessions from her feeble frightened arms. Her tiny things get swept away by streams that batter on her feet.

"Where are we going to put these things?" she cries. I fumble in the cabinet trying to find big plastic bags. The whole house rumbles.

"It's going to fall on us," she cries. "This whole thing's going down!"

I slosh in the hall where water rises on my feet, my ankles, up my calves. I feel the tough firm texture of the movement on my skin and strain against the pressing, growing current. Carrie and I wade from room to room. Our paths make crashing wakes behind us. The lights go out, then come back on. The air around moves quicker than it ever has before. The radio spits and crackles, then goes dead. I watch the water rise above my thighs, the current suck. When I drop my hold I'm swept along the hall. Then suddenly my house is huge, engulfed. The kitchen table rams against my back, lifts in a drunken sway. I knock against the wall. Chairs collide, careening down the hall. I'm tossed as if my house was loose. The water is heavy and everywhere, but nothing I can hold. I open my mouth to yell; I choke. I paw the air and stretch out desperately, then fall back again. I'm swept to my study. I can neither walk nor swim. I know that I am drowning: I remember.

I remember the brutal wet in my eyes. I remember the feeling of falling.

"Carrie," I cry, not knowing where she is.

But then I hear her voice, "Get out of there, you idiot fool, this whole thing's going down."

I turn my head to follow her voice. Her suddenly distant body waves to me from the other side of the window. She's outside calling in to me.

"Robin," she shouts through the shattered glass, "it's not outside."

I shake my head, convinced I've heard her wrong. She doesn't hear me above the deafening roar.

"It isn't falling from the sky," she screams. "It's all in there with you."

I stare at her through the sheet of falling wet, then the pane of cracked glass, and see, behind her dear soaked wringing body, dry calm sky.

"Oh God," I whisper, "Jesus, God."

I see her mouthing words to me that I can't hear. I see her face twist, desperate, crying out to me. "Get out," she yells at me, "reach me, Robin. Just get out. Just reach me, Robin, reach me."

"I can't," I whisper to myself.

"Just reach for me —" Her hand is through the ruptured glass and pushing through the waves. "This whole thing's going down," she cries.

I turn away from her and look above my desk The curtain billows forward like a skirt that's caught the wind. A crashing sound, then falling out to sprinkling. The shattered bits of glass in water shine like fallen stars.

"Oh Jesus, Robin," Carrie screams, "come with me. We can get away. The car—"

The beams that cross each other in my room drip like frosty trees in light. My sofa's peppered, tiny pricks of light, like stars, the air-puffed curtain looks like sky, all full of stars but moving. Then I hear a giant suck of air, and then the ruthless, now familiar swell of waves.

With the slow deliberate logic of a drunk, I tell myself I'll save myself by seeking out the highest place in this, my flooded room. I hoist my heavy orange armchair onto my desk and sit on it. I shiver to the snap of wood on wood, the flying shards of sharp white light, the eddies, swirls of photographs, and books.

I watch the water soak up through the soft white covers on the furniture and see the taut dark of the couch fade through. I watch the water rise and rise and rise. It never ends. I want it to finish, but it won't. No, it stays moving, motionless, and I am caught. This searing awful moment just before—

Her voice, "Get out—there's time—the whole thing's going down!"

But by the time I turn to her, I can see her no longer. The broken window's black where she once was. I shout at where I'd seen her last, her portrait in the window frame. I shout above the roaring waves, "Remember me! Forget! Remember me!" I don't know if she hears.

The water pouring down is thick full sheets. I can't see beyond my streaming eyes. The only thing I hear is sobbing floods.

I close my eyes and hope that Carrie's gone. I think of her profile next to me in the car when we drove out West, back to this place I thought I had forgotten. And I see her stricken drive from here, her lips pulled back in agony and fear, her hair pressed to her forehead, wet, her fingers tightened on the whirring wheel.

I watch the water rise around my thighs, my stomach, up my chest. I wonder if I could have gotten out. I pull my knees up to my chest and dart my eyes across my room. I watch the swirling contents of my home rush by. They flash above the surface then they sink: the movie magazines, my leather jacket. Photographs, a broken toy propeller. I look up at the sagging roof, the tops of windows, dark and far, the stopgap boards we'd placed so gingerly, our childlike attempts to reconstruct this house as if no one had let it fall before.

I feel the water inching up my ankles. I shift and squat up on my chair and stretch my back up tall. Across the surface of my room, and through my home, I watch the surging water rise.

I stretch my neck and lift my face up as close as I can to the dripping ceiling, one last tiny crack of air. I smell the water in my nose. My breath begins to gurgle. The water in my ears sounds full and calm, peaceful, like a silent glider after the propeller's roar, the silent flicker, light and dark, after the film runs out. My body goes limp. And when I finally lose my last distraction, that's when finally I forget — no — I remember, just who haunts this haunted house I'm in.

About the Author

Rebecca Brown is the author of eleven books of prose published in the US and abroad. Her titles with City Lights include: THE TERRIBLE GIRLS, ANNIE OAKLEY'S GIRL, THE DOGS: A MODERN BESTIARY, THE END OF YOUTH and THE LAST TIME I SAW YOU.